LIVING A LIE

by

Elizabeth Scott

Published by

MELROSE BOOKS

An Imprint of Melrose Press Limited
St Thomas Place, Ely
Cambridgeshire
CB7 4GG, UK
www.melrosebooks.com

FIRST EDITION

Cover designed by Sean Gladwell

ISBN 978 1 906050 27 6

Printed and bound in Great Britain by:
CPI Antony Rowe, Bumpers Farm,
Chippenham, Wiltshire, SN14 6LH, UK

Dedication

For my husband, Alex, who has always encouraged me to achieve my ambitions and follow my dreams.

1

Early Days

James Bolton stood in his room with his back to the main office, his hands in his pockets, and gazed out of the window at another sunny day. *Two days in a row – bit of a record for Lanarkshire*, he thought cynically. *It'll probably pour from the heavens tomorrow*. He stared thoughtfully at the busy car park and wondered again about the new employee who was starting this morning. She had the personal backing of Jack Forrest, the Senior Partner, who had given James the impression, during their discussion after her interview, that Miss Robson was coming to work for them whether James liked it or not. He'd said that she came highly recommended by the recruitment agency. James hadn't been able to get her out of his head ever since then and he could do without any complications at work.

Work was his solace. It didn't just occupy his time; it was his escape. It kept him sane and kept loneliness at bay. Although her heavy make-up was off-putting, he admitted to himself that she was very attractive. The office ran smoothly and everyone got on very well together, and such an attractive young woman could only cause problems, he was sure. If the decision had been his alone, he would never have taken her on. However, he hadn't been able to give Jack a good reason for not employing her, so he had reluctantly agreed to her appointment.

I won't let him bully me like that again, he decided. He seemed to remember Jack being quite insistent about John coming to work with them a couple of years ago, too. Jack was a difficult man to say 'no' to. *Not to worry*, he promised himself, *if the new girl becomes a problem I'll get rid of her.* Other problems in his life weren't so easy to deal with, but at work he was in control, except when Jack went against him. He would have to be careful not to show too much animosity to begin with – then he would claim she was incompetent and sack her. Having made this decision, he turned back to face the office and began to think about the day ahead.

Lynsey Robson drove her little black Ka along Cadzow Street in Hamilton, Lanarkshire and turned into the car park of Forrest & Bolton, Estate Agents. The July sunshine gleamed on the glass-panelled front door of the building as she pushed it open, feeling both excited and a little apprehensive. She was on time, nothing had held her back en route, and she was wearing her favourite, softly-tailored blue trouser suit. The suit matched the colour of her eyes and contrasted well with her glossy black hair, which she wore in a short bob with a full fringe, and her reflection showed her that she looked better than she felt. First days are always difficult and she had a feeling this one was likely to be more so than most.

She was to report to Mr Bolton, who had said very little at her interview but had looked rather stern and unfriendly. John had warned her that her new boss sometimes had an abrasive manner and she should try not to take it personally.

'I'll take him as I find him,' she'd answered calmly. She wasn't inclined to accept other people's opinions, preferring to make up her own mind about new acquaintances. During the course of the interview, she had felt that James Bolton could actually be rather pleasant and charismatic if he chose to. He was 40-ish and didn't have movie star looks, being of average height and stocky build, with soft-looking fair hair and a lived-in face, but there was something rather attractive about him. He exuded an air of masculinity, which was fine from a physical point of view, but she didn't like men who were aggressive and overbearing; kindness and sensitivity appealed to her more than any other qualities. She couldn't really figure out why she liked him – she was just drawn to him for some reason.

Marcia, the receptionist, looked up as Lynsey approached the front desk. Lynsey admired her slim build and long, shiny brown ringlets. She was quite tall and elegant-looking, and as Lynsey was the petite, curvy type she was aware of a little twinge of envy. Marcia smiled easily, as most receptionists do, but there was genuine warmth behind the smile. 'Hi, Lynsey, all set for your first day?' she asked pleasantly.

'Yes. Bit nervous, though,' Lynsey answered, her Glasgow accent a little stronger than usual because she was anxious.

'I'm sure you'll be fine. I'll show you where the important things are – the loo and the kitchen – then you can come and meet the guys.' Her friendliness eased Lynsey's tension a little.

She looked around the office. She'd liked it the first time she'd seen it. In contrast to the rather old-fashioned, heavy exterior, the inside was bright and airy. The overall layout was open plan, but Marcia's desk was set at an angle in a little reception area, with a glass partition between her workstation and the rest of the office. Both Jack Forrest and James Bolton had their own rooms, which were next to each other; each had large external and interior windows. The interior windows were fitted with blinds, which meant that the occupants could see what was going on in the main office, or they could close the blinds if they wanted privacy.

'How long have you been in this area?' Marcia asked as she showed Lynsey where the coats were kept.

'Oh, not long,' Lynsey replied non-committally.

'Don't you miss the city?'

Lynsey was used to people asking her this and just said, 'Sometimes,' in reply. The truth was she had spent her 25th birthday in her new flat with John and had enjoyed it so much compared to last year's fiasco with her mother and stepfather, Tony, that she wasn't really missing her Burnside home at all. She'd left the family home about six months previously and had been staying in a tiny bedsit in Glasgow and working as a temp.

Lynsey remembered being told at her interview that there were sixteen members of staff. The 'guys' all seemed very pleasant and friendly when she was introduced to them, and even James Bolton said, 'Good morning!' politely, if a little distantly. Marcia took Lynsey over to meet the members of the team.

'This is John Smith,' she said, smiling and looking into John's eyes. Her smile wavered a little as she watched Lynsey and John shaking hands and evidently trying not to grin at each other.

Behind John sat Tim and Nick, who were around Lynsey's age, or a little older, and they exchanged appreciative looks when she came over to them. They said hello and smiled at her, and Nick even winked at her. She liked Nick on sight and Jo, who was the other secretary for the office, seemed really nice, too. She began to feel that things were going to be just fine and returned happily to her own desk to begin work. She was to be Team Secretary, so it was important for her to get on with everyone, not just one or two of the staff. She'd had enough of temporary jobs and wanted to settle in one place for a while. Being close to John was an added bonus and Lynsey was determined to make it work, especially as Jack had pushed her forward for the position.

Just before lunchtime, she took a fax over to John's desk and he asked her nonchalantly if she would like to go out for a bite to eat in the pub across the road. She hesitated, thinking of the healthy lunch she'd packed earlier, and he told her that it was an office tradition on someone's first day. He grinned confidently, knowing she wouldn't be able to resist. When Nick and Tim raised their eyebrows and exchanged looks, John suggested they both come too, and they agreed. Lynsey was aware of Mr Bolton watching them through the window of his office, and judging from his face he was none too pleased, although she wasn't sure why this should be.

'Should we invite James, too?' she asked the others, but they screwed up their faces and she presumed that was a 'no'. She slipped on her jacket (helped unnecessarily by Nick) and the four of them left the office. She was sure she could feel James Bolton glaring at their departing backs.

'I knew she was going to be trouble,' he complained to Marcia as he was walking past her desk to go out of the front door. She's already got everyone vying for her attention.'

'Early days,' Marcia assured him. 'They'll settle down once they get used to her.' However, John's reaction to Lynsey hadn't escaped her and she didn't feel quite so well-disposed towards the new girl as she had at the start of the day.

* * *

Although the morning seemed to drag a little, the afternoon passed swiftly for Lynsey. There was a great deal to learn and quite a backlog to be worked through. Every now and then she found herself glancing over towards James Bolton's office, even though she kept telling herself not to. She knew he was married and she reminded herself that he was out of bounds and that she didn't want to make a habit of becoming involved with married men. Her own interest in him puzzled her a little. He wasn't exactly forthcoming with her. Maybe that was what it was, she told herself – he was the only person ignoring her and she felt put out. Still, it was annoying and she made a determined effort to ignore him. The very fact that it was an effort was unsettling.

At 5 o'clock Lynsey left the office, thinking that it had been a mixed sort of day, not all good but certainly not bad. John turned round and winked at her as he strode over to his car, which was parked near hers. She smiled and stuck her tongue out at him. He would come over to her flat this evening and they would relax and go over the day's events together. This thought made her smile as she walked out of the door. Then her mobile rang – it was Jack.

He'd been out and about for most of the day, and on his way home he'd decided to give Lynsey a bell and find out if her first day had gone smoothly.

'How did it go then, honey?' he asked breezily. He barely listened to her answer, just laughed and said, 'Give it time, give it time. Okay if I come over to see you tonight?' It wasn't really a question, he was telling her he'd be there. She could hardly refuse. After all, he *had* bought the flat for her. She'd protested, but he'd gone ahead with it anyway. She'd made a promise to herself that she would return the cost of the flat to him once she eventually sold it. If he'd been anyone else she'd have resented his interference, but as it was, she usually just gave in gracefully. Most people did, she knew, and Jack went through life using the force of his strong personality to get his own way without anyone really being aware of being manipulated.

Across town, Jack closed his phone and bent his long lean frame to slide into the driving seat of his bright red Lamborghini. The car was his pride and joy. This was his favourite model, but it wasn't a new one and his wife had often reminded him that it wasn't fitted with an airbag. But that had never been an issue for him before, and he didn't see any reason why it should be a problem in the future. He fastened his seatbelt, then glanced in the mirror. Cool blue, intelligent eyes looked back at him. He ran his fingers through his thick brown wavy hair, which he kept under control by having it cropped very short. He had to go home and tell May he would be going out again that evening. He considered not going to see Lynsey, but he couldn't resist it.

A little sigh escaped him. If he wasn't careful, his wife would begin to suspect he was having an affair and that wouldn't do at all. He wanted to tell her everything in his own time, not blurt it out in the middle of a heated argument. He shifted uncomfortably in his seat at the thought of facing her with the truth. He was not a man who usually suffered from nervous problems, but the prospect of confessing to her always had that effect on him, making him feel as if he couldn't breathe properly. When the time came he would do it calmly and reasonably and she would understand. She *would* understand – he would make her understand. He drew in a long, slow breath and then drove off at his usual break-neck speed.

When Lynsey closed her mobile she called over to John to come round to the flat later on in the evening, when she knew Jack would have left. She was too tired for any sparring between them after coping with her first day in her new job.

2

Confrontation

Lynsey soon settled in at Forrest & Bolton and found she had no problems at all with the work. She liked her colleagues and got on well with everyone. She was aware that Nick had already formed a strong attachment to her, but she was sure she could handle it. It was just a crush, like the crush *she* had on James Bolton. She was glad James didn't seem to be aware that she felt that way about him. When he wasn't engrossed in his work or talking to clients, he paid very little attention to her except to ask work-related questions or issue instructions in that curt way of his. The thing that bothered her was that he'd begun to make little barbed comments to her, usually in front of everyone else, and was often quite sarcastic, implying that she wasn't doing her job properly.

On the Monday of her third week she was sitting at her workstation trying to get on with her work. Nick was perched on the edge of her desk, quietly asking if she would like to go out for a drink with him. She could see James glaring at them through the window of his room.

'Nick, I like you a lot, but I don't usually date guys I work with,' she told him. 'You know how it is—' she broke off as James approached them.

'Have the pair of you no work to do?' he barked.

Nick glanced up in surprise at James's tone and went back to his own seat, rolling his eyes and tilting his head towards James. Lynsey would have been smiling too if she hadn't been so annoyed. As James turned to go back to his own room, Jack appeared behind him.

'Is there a problem, Jim?' he asked.

'Nothing I can't handle,' James shot back testily.

Jack looked at Lynsey, whose lips were pursed in annoyance. He tried to defuse the atmosphere by saying, 'That's all right then,' and followed James into his room. While the two of them were conferring together, Lynsey decided she wasn't going to let this situation go on. She would speak to James about it before it got out of hand. She hadn't done anything wrong and yet he had taken against her in this way. He was undermining her confidence and making her feel inadequate. She worked on steadily, but while she waited to get things off her chest, her anger grew and by the time Jack left, favouring her with a little wink as he went out, she walked determinedly over to James's room and knocked on the door. *PMT isn't always such a bad thing*, she reflected. She wouldn't normally have been bold enough to tackle him like this. She went inside and stood facing him.

'Have I done something wrong, Mr Bolton?' she asked, trying to keep her temper under control. He seemed to find her defiance amusing and sat back in his seat, saying nothing for a few seconds. Eventually he said, 'Like what, for instance?'

'I don't know – that's why I'm asking!' she challenged him.

'When you do something wrong, you'll be the first to know,' he said softly, implying that this was inevitable. She stood in silent exasperation. Well, she had tried to clear the air. If this was the way it was going to be, she'd be wasting her time in trying to win him round. Her natural pride and stubbornness and his 'stone wall' attitude stopped her from saying any more and she went back to her own desk, feeling that she hadn't really achieved anything with him.

James sat and considered Lynsey's behaviour. Her reaction was exactly what he had wanted, but he had been quite sure she would just sit and let it build up and was quite taken aback that she had actually confronted him. He knew that it had taken some courage for her to be so outspoken and challenge him like that, and his small triumph was tinged with a little guilt and a rather inconvenient feeling of admiration.

Tim watched Lynsey walking back to her desk.

'What's up?' he asked her.

'What do you mean?' she asked, frowning.

'You've got a face like a smacked behind!' he told her, making an attempt to copy her expression. In spite of her mood, she couldn't help laughing and everyone else joined in. Throughout the rest of the morning, Nick and Tim kept everyone amused with their light-hearted banter. They were like a double act sometimes and even had joint nicknames – Ant and Dec. Nobody was very sure who was supposed to be which, and the two of them took great delight in sighing and correcting their colleagues by saying, 'I'm Ant, not Dec,' and vice versa, producing even more laughter. Lynsey was very glad they were there. The office was a much happier place when they were around. James Bolton would often complain that there was too much hilarity going on when they were in full flow, but everyone knew that the work still got done as it should, and it was good for morale.

Nick and Tim went off to get some food at lunchtime, but Lynsey and John decided to stay in. James was having a rather animated conversation with a client in his room. Lynsey and John sat together, talking and eating sandwiches at their desks in the main office, which was empty except for Marcia. 'What's his problem, John?' she asked, glancing in the direction of James's room. 'I'm bending over backwards to learn the job, do things right, be pleasant – and he's blocking me at every turn, making me look bad in front of everyone. Am I missing something here?'

'Look, Lynsey, I told you, James is just moody sometimes. Doesn't have a happy home life.'

'My heart bleeds. If I let my personal life interfere with my work he'd be down on me like a ton of bricks. He gets away with it because he's in charge. It's not fair.'

'He's okay once you get used to him. Give him time, he'll come round. When you meet his other half you'll understand. She's a witch.'

'Huh, a saint more like, living with an old grouch like him!'

'Whatever. Let's go for a drink after work and James can go hang.'

Lynsey looked unsure and John gave her a quick hug, trying to reassure her.

'There's always one fly in the ointment, isn't there?' he said. 'But things are going fine apart from that.'

'Oh yes, my boss can't stand me, but that's just a minor glitch. No problem really.'

He put his forehead against hers and she sighed deeply, trying to calm down a little. James Bolton watched them surreptitiously over his client's shoulder. He was not alone in watching them. From her position in the office, Marcia could see them, too, and she swallowed, trying not to mind so much. She'd never experienced jealousy before, not like this. It made her feel torn in two – angry and sad at the same time. She wasn't going to let him treat her like this – she would have to have it out with him. *The sooner the better*, she thought miserably. She'd hardly seen him since Lynsey had arrived on the scene. She had started off really liking the girl, but it was quite obvious that John did, too. Hugging her in the office like that, right in front of her! She gritted her teeth. *She* was supposed to be his girlfriend.

She hated arguments and it would be difficult to confront John because she had been so sure that he was the one for her. She didn't want to lose him, but there was no way she was going to be made a fool of again. She had broken off an engagement a couple of years ago because her fiancé had been seeing other girls and all her friends knew about it before she did. She wanted to trust John, but he wasn't making it easy these days. She sent him a little email saying that she needed to speak to him. She was careful to keep it light-hearted and not make it sound like an ultimatum.

He replied to it at the start of the afternoon, saying he would catch her tomorrow as he was busy that evening. She dialled his extension and when he picked up, she said 'OK fine!' and slammed the phone down. He looked over at her, knowing why she was rattled but not able to do anything about it. *She'll just have to be patient*, he told himself, but he was getting impatient, too. This situation couldn't go on. He looked at Lynsey and she smiled apologetically. She knew there was friction building up between John and his girlfriend, but she wasn't about to let him go just yet. She needed him right now because of James's antagonism and Jack's procrastination. She regretted Marcia's resentment of her, especially as she really wanted to be friends with her, but it just couldn't be helped. Not for the first time in her life, she wondered why relationships always had to be so complicated.

* * *

Finishing time on Friday arrived slowly and everyone in the office was tired and ready for a few drinks, or maybe more than a few. They decided to head for the usual pub, which they all affectionately referred to as 'The Bar', a couple of streets away in the centre of Hamilton. There were other pubs and wine bars in between, but that one was their favourite, and going there had become a bit of an office tradition.

They all went over to the cupboard to get their jackets at the same time. Marcia tried to catch John's eye, but he managed to ignore her and watched in amusement as Tim and Nick elbowed each other out of the way to help Lynsey on with her jacket. James stood looking at Lynsey. She was wearing a cream suit today with a brown blouse. It went well with her sleek, dark hair, but for some reason her hair really annoyed him. It had a slightly false look, almost like a wig. *And she can just about get away with wearing such a light colour*, he thought unkindly. *A few more pounds and she'd be rather plump. Probably run to fat when she's older*, he reflected as he pulled his raincoat on over his suit. This notion pleased him; he knew she really enjoyed being well-dressed and would not like to be limited in her choices.

'It's pouring outside, by the way,' he said smugly and watched her smile fade. His pleasure in peeving her was short-lived, however, and he turned away moodily to lead the way to the pub.

Lynsey noticed the tight expression on Marcia's face as they all walked along the road together, and signalled to John to go and speak to her. He walked faster to catch up with her and took Marcia's arm.

'Hey, babe, what's up?' he asked quietly.

'You know what's up,' she answered, not so quietly. He pulled her to a stop and let Lynsey pass by, and when everyone else had gone into the pub, he looked at her enquiringly and waited for her to speak.

'What's going on, John?'

'Nothing. I don't know what you mean.'

'I mean you and Lynsey, as you know fine and well.'

'She's a nice girl. We're mates, that's all. Don't tell me you're jealous? There's nothing to be jealous about.'

'And if I was canoodling like that in the middle of the office with a new guy, that wouldn't be a problem either then?'

'Canoodling – what's canoodling?' He couldn't help laughing, although he tried really hard not to.

'Don't do that, John, this isn't funny.'

He stopped laughing and straightened his shoulders.

Marcia wasn't about to let him off the hook that easily.

'You've become very good "mates" very fast, John.' She looked at him speculatively. She knew he'd been brought up in Glasgow, too. 'It's almost as if you knew each other before …'

'Look, we were at school together, that's all. So what?'

'You were at school together? You never said. Why didn't you just tell me that?' she asked irritably.

He drew her in close to him. He looked into her eyes and told her he loved her completely and wasn't interested in Lynsey or anyone else. Deep down she knew he was telling the truth, but somehow she didn't feel as reassured as she should have done. She still felt that there was something he wasn't telling her.

'If you don't trust me, you don't love me,' he stated, rather unfairly. He knew if the situation were reversed, he wouldn't be feeling very trusting toward her.

'I'm trying to trust you, John, but you're not making it easy.' There were tears in her eyes now and he wanted to tell her everything, but he had made a promise to Jack and he had no intention of breaking it.

'If things go on like this with you and Lynsey, John …' Marcia was tearful and he hated to see her feeling hurt when there was no need.

'Marcia, I'm not Matt. You know I wouldn't do that to you,' he reassured her. *Damn Jack and his bloody secrets*, he thought angrily. He pulled her close and kissed her firmly, hoping things wouldn't drag on like this for any length of time. *Promise or no promise*, he thought, *I'm not going to risk losing Marcia for anyone.*

3

James's Project

It was early September, and although there was still plenty of sunshine, the air wasn't so warm any more. Everyone in the office was trying to adjust to the downturn in the weather and the pressures of a heavy workload. Lynsey was sitting at her desk, daydreaming a little. A depressing time of year, she thought, with the holiday season over and the festive season still some time away. She was brought up short by James yelling at her to 'Wake up!' and send an important fax for him 'Today!'

She sighed inwardly as she put the paper through the machine. Six weeks into her new job and he was still as grouchy with her as ever. She had promised John she wouldn't take his 'abrasiveness' personally, but she couldn't help it. He didn't seem to be bad-tempered with anyone else the way he was with her.

She sometimes felt a little lonely these days, as John had started spending more time with Marcia. She had been looking forward to seeing more of him when she'd moved here and now she found herself alone most of the time when she wasn't at work. She understood that he didn't want to 'mess Marcia about', as he put it, but she hadn't made any new friends yet and was starting to think maybe she should have stayed in Glasgow. She tended to eat more when she was feeling down, and she smiled as she remembered she had a Snickers bar in her bag. She shook her head – so much for watching her weight. She checked the fax machine anxiously to make sure it was working, as it was always getting paper jams, and then she decided to make the teas and coffees. She went round all the desks, lifting cups and chatting to each person as she went.

James watched her moving round the office, smiling, and found it hard to remember what it had been like before she came. He was annoyed because his plan to make her seem incompetent had come to nothing, and he couldn't think of any other way of getting rid of her besides making her life such a misery that she would leave of her own accord. He couldn't allow her to stay, that was for sure. But she had become an integral part of the office in such a short period of time that he had no illusions about how difficult it was going to be to make her go. Not only was she smart and efficient, she had a pleasant disposition, was a good listener and was always helping people with their problems. He had tried to use this against her, dubbing her 'Little Miss Fix-It' and 'Miss Goody Two-Shoes', which he knew annoyed her.

She had a knack for getting round people and pouring oil on troubled waters, but she wouldn't get round him. He had seen through her; she was obviously involved with Jack in some way and was trying to come between John and Marcia, too. She was always sucking up to Jack whenever he appeared in the office and once he had even seen the two of them go off together in his car after work. *I'm onto you,* he thought. *You might have everyone else fooled, but I can see right through you.*

He had no difficulty in believing the worst of Lynsey, but he still found it hard to believe that Jack really was involved with her. He'd known Jack for a very long time and was only too well aware of the extent of his friend's feelings for his wife. He had met him when they were both at Glasgow University. Jack had been a mature student, quite a few years older than James, but they had soon formed a strong friendship, even going out on double dates together. That was how Jack had met May, while James was dating her! As soon as Jack and May met each other, James and everyone else had faded into the background, as far as they were concerned. James had never forgotten how it had felt to watch his girlfriend and his mate fall for each other. Fortunately, he hadn't been emotionally involved enough to hold it against them and had even been Best Man at their wedding. Whenever James looked back on those times, he wondered if a residual feeling of guilt had prompted Jack to ask him to come in as a partner with him when he'd set up in the real estate business, which he had started up with funding from his wealthy parents.

James sighed then and his thoughts turned to John. Until recently they'd been good friends. For years, the two of them had spent many an evening drinking together after work. Although there was a substantial age gap, they got on well, viewed the world in the same way, and had a similar sense of humour. Everything was different now, though. It wasn't John's relationship with Marcia that bothered James. He was happy for both of them, but John didn't talk to him much any more. He had been distant with him, even at work, ever since Lynsey had arrived, and was always defending her whenever James tried to bring her down. James missed his company, and God knows, he needed some company. With a non-event of a marriage and only one 18-year old child who didn't seem to need him any more, there was nothing but work in his life except for his friendships with Jack and John.

These thoughts made him more determined than ever to get rid of Lynsey. However, the fact that everyone else seemed to really like her made it a bit tricky. He would have to be very careful not to alienate the others by showing too much animosity. But he *would* get rid of her and get things back to the way they were before. The angst he felt every time he saw her come into the office in the morning was becoming unbearable, and he was obsessed now with removing this thorn in his side as soon as possible. He could think of nothing else every evening as he sat at home drinking his two glasses of whisky, which was the most he allowed himself during the working week.

He had even started having 'anxiety' dreams about her. He felt as though she had taken over his life, which was ridiculous. She might think herself very mature at the age of 25, but to him she was just a kid, one who needed to be taught a lesson. James Bolton was a strong, dynamic man who was used to being in charge of things, at least while he was at work. He thrived on challenges and 'Little Miss Perfect' had now, unknowingly, become his latest project.

4

Secrets

On the following Friday evening, Jack left work a little earlier than usual and drove home. He drove up the steep driveway of his luxurious Bothwell bungalow, switched off the engine and sat still for a few moments trying to prepare himself for speaking to May. As it was Friday evening the pressures of the week were over. He had promised himself he would tell her and he fully intended to do so. With Lynsey being in such close proximity now, coming clean seemed more urgent, which had been his intention in asking her to move nearer to him. She was trying not to nag him, he knew, but it was there between them, unspoken, all the time. He didn't know which was worse, the thought of confessing or the thought of not being able to – again. After more than twenty-six years of being happily married to May, he still wasn't sure of the effect his words would have on her, other than causing a great deal of hurt. His stomach churned and he breathed deeply and tried to steady his heartbeat as he opened the car door.

He strode purposefully indoors, but as soon as he saw his wife, he knew he couldn't do it. His heart sank and the usual headache started, the inevitable result of the built-up tension in his neck. May kept talking all the time, almost as if she sensed he was about to tell her something unpleasant. It would just have to wait. He would do it at a time when it felt right. After all, it wasn't something you could just drop into the conversation. Lynsey would understand – she was a very understanding person.

When Jack closed his eyes and began to rub the back of his neck, May relaxed and stopped babbling. She had suspected that he was having an affair for some time now. She didn't know herself why she didn't want him to spill the beans. Was it just avoidance, she wondered? If he didn't say the words, then it wasn't really happening? She wanted to find out more about the woman he was seeing before he actually told her about it. She had heard him call her 'Lynsey' on the phone one night just before he went out, supposedly to see a client, and she wondered if it was someone from work. *It might be just a passing thing*, she thought hopefully. If she could speak to this woman and tell her how much her husband meant to her, maybe she would back off. May had no children, so Jack was her whole life and she wasn't prepared to lose him because of one slip-up. Until now, she had been certain that he was as faithful to her as she had always been to him.

It's strange, she thought, *how actually being in a situation can make you behave quite differently from the way you always imagined you would in those circumstances.* She had always believed that if ever Jack was unfaithful to her, she would no longer feel anything for him and would immediately tell him to leave and then start divorce proceedings. She had said as much to him several times over the years. Perhaps she'd known, deep down, that he would eventually stray.

Her friends had warned her before they married that he was well named, as he was known to be quite a 'Jack the Lad'. Even Jim had warned her about Jack's reputation with women, and he was Jack's friend. Maybe, also, she felt a little guilty for not having been able to give him children. They'd both had fertility tests within a few months of marrying, as Jack was not a patient man and wanted to start a family as soon as possible. But when he'd found out she could never have a child he had stood by her. They'd had a good life together. She had held things together for this long and she knew that, deep down, he loved her as much as she loved him. Generally speaking, she felt that unfaithful men were not worth fighting for, and yet, now that the situation was happening to her, that was exactly what she intended doing.

Jack went off to his den to speak privately on his mobile, and there wasn't much doubt in her mind who was on the other end of the line.

* * *

As it was a Friday evening, James Bolton and most of the others in the office headed for The Bar, as usual. Lynsey hadn't really wanted to go, but John had persuaded her.

'I don't like drinking on an empty stomach,' she'd complained. 'Can't we go for something to eat first?'

'Like where, for instance? If we go somewhere for food it'll take us ages to get served and then we'll have to stand all night when we get to the pub,' John had pointed out. 'You'll be fine once you've had a few,' he'd added unhelpfully. She wasn't convinced and trailed a little behind him and Marcia. Then Tim and Nick caught up with her and she chatted brightly to them so as not to feel left out. Nick didn't seem to bear her a grudge after she had turned down the date with him and she was glad of that. She wasn't sure if he believed that it was because they worked together, or if he suspected she was interested in someone else. At any rate, he and Tim were fun to be with, and she tried to ignore the pangs of hunger and look forward to some pleasant, uncomplicated company.

As the evening wore on, James watched his colleagues relax as the alcohol had the desired effect, and there was a great deal of laughter, especially from the corner where Lynsey, Nick and Tim were sitting. James had only had one pint, as he was driving, but he fully intended to make up for lost time once he got home. He noticed that Lynsey kept looking over at John and Marcia. When Lynsey went into the Ladies, Nick and Tim both looked over at James and he knew they were discussing him.

'What's up with James these days?' Tim asked.

'What do you *think*'s up with him, you plank?' Nick said, giving Tim an exasperated look. 'He's smitten with Lynsey, isn't he?'

Tim snorted. 'If that was it, he'd be nice to her, wouldn't he, not bitin' her head off all the time.'

'You sure your name's Tim? Shouldn't it be Dim? He hasn't got a prayer with her, has he? Durr…'

'Oh … right,' Tim said, then added, 'Why not?'

'Well now, let me see, oh yeah right – he's married, for one—'

'That's never stopped him before!' interrupted Tim.

'Two,' Nick continued, more loudly, 'he's nearly old enough to be her father. Three, he's her boss, and four—', he bent his head and whispered, 'she's got the hots for John, in case you hadn't noticed! And by the way, those two over there are well up for it. Come on, we're in there!' They moved over to the bar to try their luck with some giggling women who were obviously on a girls' night out and had been looking across at them all evening.

When she sat down in her seat again, Lynsey saw Tim and Nick making their move on the girls and she picked up her glass and tried not to mind being on her own. She finished her drink and decided it was time to leave. Then Marcia went to the Ladies and John came over to talk to Lynsey. The two of them still had their heads together when Marcia came back out, unnoticed by either of them. John touched Lynsey's cheek as a goodbye gesture, then stood up to meet Marcia's dark, angry eyes.

'I warned you, John!' she yelled. 'I've had enough. It's over!' So saying, she barged out of the front door.

'Go after her, John,' Lynsey said urgently. 'Go on!'

'And tell her what, exactly – about us?'

'You have to do something, John. Please go after her.'

'There's no point,' he said quietly. 'It'll just happen again, anyway.'

John and Lynsey left the pub together and shared a taxi home. Marcia stood, unseen, at the end of the street, watching them through her tears. A few moments later James left the pub, too. He was preoccupied and almost didn't notice her standing there. Then he went over and asked her if she needed a lift home. The anger he felt towards Lynsey was growing stronger by the moment.

5

Marcia's Problem

John had thought he could cope with Marcia's decision, but he soon realised he couldn't. As the weeks passed and autumn became winter, he missed her badly, even though he saw her every day. By November he was really miserable. *It won't be for long*, he kept telling himself, but visions of her taking up with someone new plagued him until he felt he couldn't stand it. He turned to Lynsey more and more, but Marcia ignored them, seeming to have washed her hands of him. He thought she looked miserable herself. Her face was thinner and paler and she was definitely losing weight she couldn't afford to lose. Lynsey had noticed this, too, and had asked Marcia a couple of times if she was all right.

'I'm fine,' she'd answered stiffly, but she'd looked away as she'd said it and Lynsey had had to let it go. Whatever it was, she obviously didn't want to talk about it.

James was now being an absolute pig to her all the time. She presumed it was because he blamed her for what had happened between John and Marcia. He took every opportunity to be rude to her and make her look small in front of everyone. She wanted to shout at him that it wasn't her fault.

A couple of days later she actually did say that to him, when he came over to her to complain about the fax again.

'It's not my fault,' she said recklessly.

'No, it wouldn't be your fault, would it, Miss Goody Two-Shoes? Little Miss Innocent. Nothing's ever your fault, is it? Well, let me tell you something.' He bent down and whispered maliciously, 'Everything was fine till you came here. Why don't you just go back where you came from – nobody wants you here.'

His words stung and tears came into her eyes. She said, loudly but shakily, 'Everything wasn't fine. A lot of things weren't fine at all.' But she got no further because Jack appeared behind her and the sudden silence in the room told her that everyone was now listening to them.

'Can I speak to you for a moment, James?' Jack asked, deceptively calmly. Lynsey tried to speak, but Jack cut her off.

'I need to discuss this with Jim, please, Lynsey.'

James marched into Jack's room with a poker-straight back and clenched jaw, determined not to back down. Lynsey left the room and went into the Ladies. She sat down inside one of the cubicles, trying to calm herself down. She could hear someone being sick in another cubicle. Once the woman had washed her face and hands, she left the Ladies and Lynsey opened her cubicle door in time to catch a glimpse of Marcia's distinctive stiletto heels as the door closed behind her.

In his own room, Jack sighed and asked James to sit down. James sat down heavily, his face tight, and glared at his friend.

'I realise you and Lynsey aren't getting along, James, but I've asked you to accommodate her as a personal favour to me and you seem to be doing the opposite.'

'I don't see any reason why I should "accommodate" someone who's caused nothing but trouble since she came here.' James suspected he knew the reason perfectly well, but he wanted Jack to confirm it.

'What sort of trouble has she caused, James?'

'She's disrupted everybody's lives – everything's changed now. John and Marcia have split up and me and John hardly speak to each other any more. Marcia hates her and so do I.'

'Then I suggest that in future you all leave your personal problems at home when you come into the office. And that's an order!'

James was so stunned and angry he got up and left Jack's room without saying another word. Jack had, unintentionally, just made the situation a great deal worse for Lynsey.

When Lynsey was summoned to James's room as soon as she came back to her desk, Marcia's problems faded into the background as her boss informed her in no uncertain terms that 'having friends in high places' didn't impress him.

'What have I done wrong?' she demanded.

'You *know*!' he said, as he invariably did when she asked him that question.

'If I knew, I wouldn't have to ask, would I?' she replied. She was getting exasperated now and frustration was stoking up her temper.

'Me and Jack and May go back a long way,' he told her. 'I won't stand by and do nothing while you wreck their marriage. You're nothing but a gold-digger, Miss Butter Wouldn't Melt, so don't come the innocent with me.'

'I don't know what you're talking about,' she said, more hesitantly, beginning to worry that she knew only too well what he suspected.

'You know all right,' he said again.

'If you say that to me one more time … oh, I'm just not having this conversation any more,' she said, at the end of her tether. 'I'm just not doing it.' She was on the verge of tears, but James noticed that the righteous indignation had gone.

She left his room in disgust and tried to switch off mentally from dwelling on her problems with James so that she could work out whether or not to tell John what she thought she knew about Marcia.

* * *

The following morning, Lynsey followed Marcia into the Ladies and stood tidying her hair in front of the mirror until she heard the girl trying to be sick again. Marcia's stomach seemed to be completely empty this morning and she was retching painfully. Lynsey stared at her reflection in the mirror and her hand stopped midway through brushing her hair as she came to the conclusion that she was right about Marcia's problem. The quandary Lynsey found herself in now was whether or not to tell John about the situation.

When Marcia came out of the cubicle, she tried to avoid Lynsey's eyes. 'I've got a tummy bug,' she lied. Lynsey nodded and turned away, thinking that if that were really the case, she'd be off work, not trying to pretend she was fine.

* * *

That evening, when John came over to Lynsey's flat, she poured drinks for them both, handed him his glass and sat down. John was sitting staring into space, drinking slowly. She hesitated, then said, as calmly as she could, 'John, I think Marcia might be pregnant.'

He turned to look at her in shock but said nothing.

'Now, I'm not sure, so don't go taking it as gospel. It's just a suspicion. I could be wrong.'

He put down his drink and, surprisingly, his face relaxed into a smile as he got up, came over to her and gave her a big bear hug.

'John, I might be totally wrong, it's just a feeling,' she said innocently.

'I don't care,' he said, 'It's just the excuse I need to sort things out with her, and that's exactly what I'm going to do – right now!'

'But John—'

He turned at the door. 'I don't care, Lynsey, I can't stand any more of this,' he said, and was gone before she could argue. She smiled to herself and crossed her fingers. Then she bit her lip as she thought of the promise she knew John would have to break. *Well, what else could I do?* she reassured herself. She shrugged and refilled her glass.

6 Resolution

Marcia tried to close the door in John's face when she saw him standing on her doorstep, but he was expecting that reaction and put his foot forward quickly to prevent the door closing.

'Go away and leave me alone' she yelled. Her flatmate, Tracey, came up behind her and asked what the problem was. When she saw John she raised her eyebrows, then she turned to Marcia.

'If you really want rid of him I'll get the police,' she said, 'but what harm can it do to talk to him? If the two of you talk and you still want him to leave, I can call the police then.' She looked enquiringly at Marcia, who stood back and reluctantly opened the door to let him in. As they moved into Marcia's room, her flatmate put on her jacket, and as soon as they closed the door behind them, she slipped out of the front door and left them to it. They obviously had some serious talking to do.

Marcia stood with her arms folded across her chest and a closed look on her face. John thought it best to start with the bottom line.

'Will you marry me, Marcia?' he asked, swallowing nervously.

Her jaw dropped. When she recovered from the unexpected proposal, she answered him tentatively.

'Why – because I'm pregnant?' she said at last. 'I won't marry a man I can't trust, John,' she added.

She knew that Lynsey would have told John of her suspicions, and she was pleased that he had come to sort things out with her, but she wasn't going to hand it to him on a plate. She had to make him understand that he would have to play it straight down the line with her. She also wanted to know that it was her he wanted; he wasn't just doing this because of a sense of duty.

John took in the closed expression on her face and silently cursed his father for putting him in this position. He knew if he played fast and loose with her trust now he would never get it back again completely, but he was starting to get really annoyed by her attitude. He wanted her blind trust and she obviously wasn't about to give that to him. He began to wonder if she felt as strongly about him as he did about her. He realised then that she'd never really recovered from Matt's betrayal and he wasn't going to live under a cloud that wasn't even of his own making. If she wasn't prepared to give any ground, there was no future for them.

'I'll take that as a "no" then?' he asked angrily, his jaw clenched in annoyance.

'You can take it whatever way you want,' she told him stubbornly, masking her disappointment with coldness.

'Shit, Marcia, why are you doing this to us?' he asked pleadingly.

'It takes two to tango,' she said, fighting to hold back her tears.

'What the hell does that mean?'

'It means,' she ground out, 'that both of us brought about this situation, but it's up to me to sort it out.'

'Marcia, you wouldn't …' he said disbelievingly. 'Don't, please. You know I love you. We can work things out.'

'I don't think we can, John. I think it's too late for us.'

'You can't mean that!'

'I want you to go now,' she told him, struggling to keep from breaking down in front of him.

'Marcia, don't do anything rash. We can talk again later when we've both calmed down.'

'I'm perfectly calm,' she lied, opening the door for him to leave.

'Promise me we'll talk about this tomorrow!'

'Fine. We'll talk about it tomorrow.'

He moved slowly out of the door.

'I'll call you.'

'OK. See you.'

She closed the door and locked it behind him.

* * *

The following day Marcia didn't come in to work and John was very grouchy all day. Lynsey tried to speak to him, but he was just too preoccupied to pay any attention to her.

'Did you sort things out with her, John?' she asked him when he finally seemed to be listening.

'Not exactly,' he answered cryptically.

'Well, either you did or you didn't, which is it?'

He didn't reply.

'John—'

'When the Debating Society have quite finished their discussion, could we have some work done in here, please,' James Bolton's sarcastic voice drawled, interrupting their conversation.

Lynsey sent John an email saying that they could continue their discussion after work. He shrugged his shoulders without turning round.

At the end of the day, John dialled Marcia's number and she answered on the first ring. He asked if he could come over to her place and she told him there was no need, that the problem was dealt with. After a stunned silence, he said, "What do you mean, Marcia – dealt with?' His blood ran cold as he waited for her reply.

'I mean it's over – I've had a termination – today.'

The receiver slipped out of his hands and his jaw dropped. He was stunned and horrified.

'I can't believe this!' he said, over and over, unable to take it in.

Lynsey had been putting on her coat whilst he was speaking to Marcia and she came over to ask him what was wrong. When he told her she shook her head in disbelief.

'No, she wouldn't, John. Marcia wouldn't do that. She wouldn't.'

'Well, she bloody has!' he yelled at her. 'She has! Oh God, she has!'

He stood up and ran out of the door. Lynsey ran after him. James Bolton had been watching the exchange from his room. He locked up the office and followed them outside.

'Wait, John, wait!' Lynsey begged him, pulling on his sleeve.

'What the hell for?' he barked, pulling his arm out of her grasp.

He took off again and she knew he was going to storm round to Marcia's to have it out with her.

She was right. He reached her flat in record time. The drive had done nothing to calm his spirit and he banged on her door constantly until she opened it. He barged in and stood looking at her in a belligerent rage. He was so angry he couldn't speak.

'Still want to marry me, John?' she asked quietly.

He took a moment to answer.

'I didn't propose to you because you were pregnant. I asked you to marry me because I love you.' His voice broke and he bowed his head as the anger gave way to pain.

'I can't believe you've done this thing,' he told her. 'Why did you? Why? Because you think I'm interested in Lynsey?'

'No matter what you say, John, I've seen the way you look at her. I can see the love in your eyes, you can't hide it from me. You don't want it to be true, but it *is* true. You love her!'

He had a momentary stab of guilt from the knowledge that this wouldn't have happened if he had confided in her. He opened his mouth to tell her the truth, but then decided that she didn't deserve to know the truth. Let her find out later, when everyone else did. She hadn't given him a chance to explain things, so he wasn't going to.

'Yes, I do love Lynsey,' he said softly, 'and I'll never forgive you for what you've done!'

The look on her face told him he had his revenge. He turned on his heel and left without another word.

Lynsey watched him leave Marcia's flat, and once he was gone she went over to the door and turned the handle. The door opened and she went inside. There was total silence as she walked along the hall to the kitchen. It was empty, but she could hear Marcia in the bathroom opposite. She was being violently sick. Lynsey wasn't sure how ill a woman would feel after an abortion, or if it was just a nervous reaction to the confrontation with John. She was also aware that there was a third possibility.

Lynsey understood how both Marcia and John were feeling right now, and she realised that they were both proud and stubborn and would probably have quite a stormy relationship ahead of them, if they even managed to get back together again. Still, they loved each other, that was the important thing, and she was thoroughly sick of being the person coming between them. Jack had had his chance to speak up. Now it was her turn.

When the other girl emerged from the bathroom, deathly pale, the two young women stood and stared at each other. Lynsey was the first to speak.

'Marcia, whether or not you've had a termination, there's something you need to know about me and John.'

Marcia took a deep breath and steeled herself for what was to come. Lynsey told her that John was her brother. Marcia swayed a little as though she was going to faint, then she burst into tears. As she sobbed, Lynsey went over to her and put her arm around her shoulder.

* * *

Lynsey stayed with her until she felt stronger.

'Do you want the doctor to come?' she asked.

'No, I'm fine.' Marcia answered, taking a deep breath and beginning to feel calmer. Then she smiled and said, 'We're both fine.' Lynsey smiled back at her.

'I'm glad you didn't go to the clinic,' she told her, 'and I understand why you told John you had. You were calling his bluff and he was so angry he did what you expected him to do. But put yourself in his position for a moment, Marcia. You'd have done the same thing in his shoes. But that doesn't mean he doesn't love you. You do know that, don't you?'

Marcia nodded miserably.

'He said he'd never forgive me,' she whispered, her lip trembling.

'Heat of the moment,' Lynsey promised her. 'I'll talk to him once he's calmed down a bit! You get some rest, Marcia, and I'll sort things out. With hindsight, I should have done this sooner,' she added ruefully.

She gave Marcia a comforting squeeze and headed off home. It would be Saturday tomorrow and that would be soon enough to deal with John, she decided.

7 Suspicions

The following morning, Lynsey asked John to come and see her. He was obviously still angry and upset, but he eventually agreed to come over.

As soon as he came in the door she said, 'John, I've told Marcia.'

'Told her what?' he asked, looking at her cautiously.

'About us. It wasn't right to keep her in the dark. It's not your fault, you promised Jack and you didn't want to break your promise, I know that.'

He shrugged his shoulders.

'Well, I don't see what was the point of doing that. It's over between us anyway.'

She sighed heavily.

'John, you're even more stubborn than her! You know it isn't over.'

'She got rid of our child, Lynsey. You can't expect me to just forget that,' he said, clenching his jaw tightly. 'She obviously doesn't trust me, so there's no more to be said.'

'Go over there and tell her you want her back, child or no child, that's all she wants to hear,' Lynsey said, trying not to get exasperated. She wouldn't break Marcia's confidence unless she had to.

'Dammit, John, you're not showing much trust in her either, are you?'

'What do you mean?' he asked, screwing his eyes up in sudden suspicion.

'I'm not saying any more, I've said enough already. Go and sort it out – now!'

He stood looking at her for a moment and then turned to go.

'And don't be aggressive with her,' she ordered tersely. Just tell her you love her and everything will work itself out from there.'

He started to speak, but she held up her hand. 'I'm not saying any more, John. It's up to you.'

He left reluctantly, a deep frown creasing his brow.

On the way to Marcia's flat, he thought about what Lynsey had said and decided that his sister was right. He did still want to be with Marcia and he always would, no matter what.

When she opened the door to him, he stood on the doorstep and said, 'Yes.'

'Yes what?' she asked him.

'Yes, I do still want to marry you,' he answered. 'I'm still mad at you, but I want to be with you and we can start a family later, when the timing is right for us.'

She blinked in total surprise and was unable to speak. He watched her eyes fill with tears and he took her in his arms and held her close. It was some time before she was able to tell him the truth about the baby. She apologised for her deception and he forgave her happily. He also made a mental note to remember how alike they were in temperament and that she could be as stubborn as he could, if she felt he wasn't being completely honest with her. He smiled wryly to himself. Life with this woman wouldn't be dull, that was for sure.

* * *

The news of John and Marcia's engagement and their prospective parenthood was the talk of the office on Monday morning. For some reason, James Bolton was more delighted than anyone else. He shook John's hand vigorously and hugged Marcia, and then he turned a look of triumph on Lynsey that really annoyed her. He seemed to sense that she had mixed feelings about the engagement and he looked at it as a point scored over her.

Lynsey, in actual fact, hadn't wanted John and Marcia to split up, and was really glad they were back together again, but their official engagement put things into a new sphere. Events would escalate now and there wasn't much she could do about it. She listened as Marcia happily told John that her parents, understandably, were keen to meet him as soon as possible. It was obvious to Lynsey that he had told Marcia everything would be out in the open soon, which wasn't really the situation just yet. He looked put out. 'Can you put them off for a while?' he asked, looking sideways at Lynsey, who rolled her eyes upwards and shook her head at him.

'Well, sometime soon then. They're dying to meet you, John'. Marcia told him, walking back to her desk.

'Haven't thought this through, have you, John?' Lynsey hissed at him quietly so as not to be overheard. 'They're going to want to know all about you – and your family.'

'It'll sort itself out,' he said unconvincingly, but a cloud had settled over his elation.

'I wouldn't bank on that happening anytime soon,' she warned.

'You were the one who got us together again!' he reminded her.

'I didn't tell you to propose to her – not right now, anyway!'

'Well, what else could I do? I love her and she's having my child – she deserves better – and I wasn't about to risk losing her.'

'Does Jack know yet?' Lynsey asked worriedly.

Before John had time to answer, James positioned himself in between the two of them. 'Have you sent that fax I gave you?' he growled at Lynsey.

'Yes, it's gone,' she said defiantly.

'Then how come they haven't received it yet?' he demanded.

'I don't know, I'll check and see,' she said in a resigned tone of voice.

'Do that!' he rasped.

She walked over to the fax machine, aware that he had once again quite deliberately disrupted her and John's conversation. She could seldom speak to anyone now without James interrupting. There was only so much she would take without losing her temper. She had too much pride to let him walk all over her like this. Then she looked over and saw John sitting with his elbow on the desk and his hand on his forehead and she knew she was being selfish. She was needed here, now more than ever. She would just have to put up with James Bolton and he would just have to get used to her being here.

A few moments later John's phone rang. As he listened to the caller, he made an anxious face at her and she realised it was Jack on the line. When John's responses began to get heated Lynsey signalled to him to transfer the call to her. After a moment he did so and she picked up her extension. She thought the best thing to do was to arrange to meet him and talk things through. Just as she was saying, 'OK, see you at five then, Jack', James passed by her desk and came to an abrupt halt as she put the phone down.

'Was that Jack Forrest you were arranging to meet?' he asked incredulously.

'Of course not,' she lied, but she was blushing furiously, so she couldn't say anything else with any credibility. He bent down to speak savagely right in her ear.

'You must think I zip up the back!' Then he marched off and slammed the door of his room.

She was really worried now. He couldn't have guessed about her and Jack, surely? But if he had, then why was he so angry about it? Jack would kill her if he thought she'd said anything. *Well*, she thought, *he'll just have to talk to May really soon, for everyone's sake*. She would have to impress this on him strongly when they met. She put her hands up to her hot face. It was beginning to cool down at last, but her credibility with James Bolton was at an all-time low and she was sure he wasn't going to just let it go. *Jack, you're going to wonder what's hit you when I see you*, she promised herself.

James sat down at his desk and picked up the phone with determination. Working on a hunch, he was going to do some property research that wasn't directly connected with work. He intended to find out who owned Lynsey's flat. He remembered reading her CV and wondering how she could afford to live where she did, alone, on her salary. If his suspicions turned out to be correct, he decided he would do a further bit of sleuthing and follow Lynsey after work to see if she and Jack met up. Then he'd know for sure.

* * *

Jack picked her up from the corner of the street after work. She'd waited until everyone else had gone and had looked carefully around as she walked along the road, to make sure she wasn't being watched. She climbed into his car and leaned over to kiss him before he drove off.

She didn't see James's car parked in a crowded side street. He'd ducked down below the windscreen as she passed him, hoping that she wouldn't notice the car at all. He'd left work about ten minutes previously, but he'd noticed her hanging back waiting for everyone else to leave and he knew she was going to meet *him*, after that phone call this afternoon. He needed to know for sure that there was something going on between them, so he'd left the car park and driven round the corner. Jack's car arrived within a few minutes, but James still waited, just to be sure he wasn't jumping to conclusions. He couldn't help hoping that there was another explanation apart from the obvious one. When she kissed Jack, his suspicions were confirmed, and he was aware of feeling a whole host of emotions churning inside him. He would have to consider his options, he decided. No point in cutting off his nose to spite his face. *Why did it have to be Jack, of all people?* he thought despairingly. The pictures he was getting in his head were more than a little disturbing. He began to feel a deep rage curling inside him and rationalised it by telling himself it was because Jack and May were old friends of his. He was determined *she* wouldn't destroy their marriage. He would just have to work out how best to get rid of her, other than killing her, which was the option that seemed to appeal to him most at that moment in time. He decided to follow them for a little distance, so that there would be no doubt in his mind of the nature of their relationship.

* * *

James wasn't the only one struggling to control his emotions. Lynsey was trying to keep calm, but was determined to put across the urgency of the situation to Jack, when he said, 'I know, Lynsey, I know. I wish to God I'd just told her about it all in the first place, but I was too scared of losing her. I still am. And I *am* trying, it's just so hard.'

She sighed and said 'I know, it must be, but with John and Marcia getting engaged …'

'I've been trying to do this for over a year, ever since I decided I can't keep it from her any longer, but I keep getting cold feet just as I'm about to tell her – it happens every time. I don't know how to get round it.'

'Can't you tell her some other way?'

'What, like write her a letter, send her an email, phone her?' He glared at her as if she were crazy.

'There must be some way.'

He shook his head. 'No, there isn't. I'll just have to bite the bullet.'

'But what if you can't, Jack, where does that leave us? It wasn't meant to take so long. It should have been over by now. You know, things are getting quite awkward in the office as well – with me and James.'

'What's James got to do with it?'

She sighed. 'I don't know. I've just got a feeling he thinks we're carrying on.'

He drew the car to a sudden stop and snorted. 'He thinks we're having an affair?' he asked, shaking his head in disbelief.

'Don't be ridiculous, Lynsey. Anyway, he's never even seen us together, we've been careful. And even if he did see us together, he wouldn't immediately jump to that conclusion!'

'OK, Jack, what do you think May would think if she saw us together now?'

'Huh, May knows I'd never—' he broke off as he realised what he was about to say, and she looked steadily at him. He covered his face with his hands and closed his eyes.

'What am I going to do? It's driving me mad. I can't do it to her, I just can't. What am I going to do?'

She put her arms around him and held him gently, her anger and agitation melting into sympathy as she imagined how she would feel in his situation. *Not that I'd ever get myself into this kind of situation*, she promised herself.

'You know I would speak to her for you, if you wanted. You only have to say.'

'It'll be bad enough coming from me, Lynsey. I can't let her hear it from anyone else.'

They sat holding each other for some time, neither of them able to see any way out of what was becoming an increasingly desperate situation.

In his own car, a few yards behind them, James Bolton clenched his teeth, did a U-turn and drove home.

* * *

James's behaviour towards Lynsey worsened considerably during the next few weeks. He was now treating her with open hostility and berated her for little or no reason in front of the rest of the office at every opportunity.

He had become aware that although she was fairly assertive in her manner on a one-to-one basis, she did not like speaking in public, and was in fact almost phobic about it, and he used this against her whenever he could.

Usually, when the office held its monthly staff meeting, it was up to each individual whether or not they wished to contribute anything. But during the meeting at the end of November, James had been speaking about the new filing system they had introduced, which Lynsey was overseeing, and he suddenly turned to her and asked her to give them all a summary of the thinking behind the new system.

She stared at him in horror and said nothing. Everyone was staring at her, waiting for her to speak. She could feel a deep flush creeping up her neck and face, and although she tried to speak, no words came out of her mouth. It was similar to stage fright – she just clammed up and couldn't say anything. She was mortified and also very angry at James, who had given her no warning that he was going to ask her to speak. She looked at John, who was glaring at James. John said that they were running out of time and maybe Lynsey could type up a description of the changes to the filing system for them all to read instead. She thanked him with her eyes and swallowed hard, then she looked down at the table so that she couldn't see if anyone was still looking at her.

James gave a self-satisfied little smirk and took a moment to answer, condescendingly, 'Yes, perhaps that would be best.'

The meeting broke up and Lynsey was through the door and out of the Board Room before anyone else. She headed straight for the Ladies. She could hear Marcia behind her, asking if she was OK. She ran into the first cubicle and locked the door. She tried to take deep breaths, but all she wanted to do was cry. She was determined not to, because then he would know how much he'd upset her, so she didn't answer Marcia when she tried to get her to come out. Eventually Marcia left her alone and she emerged from the cubicle and looked at her reflection in the mirror.

Her face was very pale and there were red blotches all over her face and throat. She knew from past experience that it would take some time for these to disappear, so she leaned against the wall with her eyes closed, preparing to wait it out. After five minutes or so, Marcia came into the Ladies again. Lynsey asked her if she would bring her handbag to her and when she came back with it Lynsey smiled at her gratefully. She took out her make-up case and began to smooth foundation onto her face and neck. Then she popped a little herbal pill into her mouth to help her relax. She felt a little better now and her breathing had returned to normal.

Marcia was wise enough not to say anything to her and the two girls went back into the office together. Lynsey went straight over to the water cooler and poured herself a long cold drink before going back to her desk. She didn't look at anyone and simply resumed her work as if nothing had happened. Her anger and humiliation bubbled beneath her calm exterior, like a volcano about to erupt, and it was cold consolation to her to promise herself that one day James Bolton would be sorry he had declared war on her.

8

Surprise Visit

It was early December and Lynsey was keeping very quiet around the office these days. She was glad James was quiet too, as she felt she couldn't take much more 'attitude' from him. She wasn't quite at breaking point, but she wasn't far away from it. For once, he wasn't badgering her, and it gave her a little time to think. At lunchtime she walked all round the shopping precinct. She had no enthusiasm for it at the moment, but Christmas wasn't too far away and she had to start her shopping some time. She bought a little silver Christmas tree and a few decorations for the flat. Then she chose a designer silk scarf for her mother and headed back to the office.

As the recent weeks passed slowly by, she'd begun to feel that Jack would *never* speak to May about her and John. *If I could just figure out something, an easier way for him to approach May rather than just blurting it all out*, she thought. She was still engrossed in these thoughts when she walked back through the swing doors and past reception, heading for her desk. A familiar tinkly laugh made her stop in her tracks and she turned disbelievingly towards James's office. She gazed at the slim, expensively dressed woman, who was an older, thinner version of herself, except that she wore her black hair drawn back from her face in a chic chignon. The woman was smiling ingratiatingly at James, who was beaming back at her. As Lynsey marched through his open door the woman said, 'Lynsey, what on earth have you done to your hair?'

'Mother, what are you doing here?' Lynsey squeaked

'I'm chatting to your *very* nice boss,' the woman drawled. 'No wonder you've been hiding him, Lynsey.' she said, giving James a suggestive look. 'I would, too,' she added cheekily. Lynsey felt very put out. Her mother was blatantly flirting with James and he was flirting back! She realised it was the first time she had ever seen him smiling! Anxious in case John or Jack would appear, and eager to end the conversation, Lynsey grabbed her mother by the arm and drew her out of the room towards the reception area.

'See you later, Julia!' James called out as they left his room.

'Why did you come here to my work?' Lynsey asked again.

'I wanted to arrange to come see you at Christmas time and I couldn't get hold of you,' Julia complained. 'That's what happens when you don't let me know where you're staying. I had to look up the office address in the phone book!' she said accusingly, pouting.

Lynsey sighed heavily. 'OK, what's happened now?'

'It's Tony, darling. He's left me. I've got no one now! I'm all alone!'

'So what, mother, I'm alone, too,' Lynsey pointed out rather sharply.

'Well, you don't have to be, you can always come back home.'

'I'm settled here now, I've got a flat in Uddingston,' Lynsey told her.

'I don't want to be on my own – it's nearly Christmas. I thought maybe I could come over and we could have lunch together somewhere. What do you think? Could we?' Julia was using her best wheedling tone and her eyes were round and hopeful.

'Well, I've got the work's Christmas do on Friday, but you could come over on Saturday and stay overnight.'

Julia was so pleased that Lynsey began to feel quite guilty for not having invited her sooner, but still she found herself sighing.

Having her mother around usually spelt trouble. *Maybe she's mellowed a bit by now*, Lynsey thought hopefully. She couldn't very well send her off home now that she had made an effort to come and see her, so she suggested that Julia do some shopping and then wait for her in the café just along the street until finishing time. That would keep her from coming into the office again. Quite apart from the possibility of her bumping into Jack, Lynsey didn't want her talking to James again. She felt infuriated every time she remembered him kissing the back of Julia's hand and Julia simpering and batting her eyelashes at him. It didn't bear thinking about! She went back into the building and stomped over to her desk, turning her back on James but feeling his eyes on her.

Her mother was an irrepressible flirt and obviously James was, too. Now she gave more credence to his reputation as a ladies man. Her mother, for heaven's sake. *It's disgusting*, she thought furiously, striking the keys so fast she didn't even know what words she was typing.

James could see she was rattled, so he came over to her desk, smiling, and said:

'What a lovely woman your mother is, Lynsey. Who'd have thought it?'

She turned to face him, her jaw clenched, but she said nothing, trying not to rise to his obvious baiting.

'I can see now where you get your looks. Shame about the personality,' he said nastily.

She watched him head off to see a client and was glad he couldn't see her face. *If he was any good at lip reading I'd be out of a job*, she thought.

'Things not any better with Jim, then?' John asked unnecessarily.

'Never mind him – what's happening with you and Marcia?' she answered. 'Are you going to meet her family at the weekend?'

'Yeah.'

'Better mind your p's and q's then,' she warned.

'Yeah,' he said again, wearily.

* * *

Julia Robson did some window shopping for a couple of hours, but she didn't go to the café afterwards, as Lynsey had suggested – she preferred the atmosphere in the pub. She tapped her cigarette in the ashtray, sipped her wine and crossed her legs, watching out of the corner of her eye as the youngish man serving behind the bar tried not to look as though he was checking her out. She had always had that effect on men, since she was 14 years old. Although she was used to male attention, it was still important to her, and she knew it probably always would be. Even when she eventually grew old she was quite determined she would never look her age or be down-at-heel or frumpy. She had watched other women letting themselves go in that way, but that wouldn't do for her.

Also, she had a special reason for keeping herself attractive – even after all these years she had never quite given up on the idea of getting back together with Jack Forrest. She had only gone through with her pregnancy in the belief that he would leave his barren wife for her. He'd left her in no doubt, at the time, that this would not be happening and that there would be hell to pay if she contacted May. She'd given up too easily, she knew. The man was worth a fortune, for heaven sake! And now that she was footloose and fancy-free again, well who knew what could happen if she played her cards right. She wasn't stupid. She knew why Lynsey had moved here and she knew if she hung around her daughter long enough, it was only a matter of time before Jack would show up. He must be pretty sick of his boring little wife by now, she was sure. Most men just needed a little push in the right direction. The rest was up to her. She smiled to herself as she headed off to meet her daughter. *And it wouldn't do any harm to flirt a little with Lynsey's very sexy boss in the meantime, would it?* she thought as she watched him come through the door of the building.

As she moved towards him, Lynsey appeared from behind him, grabbed Julia's arm and said hurriedly,

'Mother, you must come and see my flat. What would you like for tea? We'll pick something up on the way home.' So saying, she drew her away so that she and James wouldn't have a chance to talk again.

* * *

Later on in the evening the wine started to run out and Julia began complaining to Lynsey.

'Darling, I can't believe that's all the wine you've got in the house! How *do* you manage?'

'Oh, I get by somehow,' Lynsey answered drily, trying to prepare the food and count slowly to ten at the same time.

'Jack did you proud with the flat anyway, love. You know, if you're ever short, I'm sure he —'

'Mother, I can manage on my own,' Lynsey snapped.

'Of course you can, dear, but I just mean that there's no need to go without things, is there? By the way, does he come by to see you often?'

'Sometimes,' Lynsey replied non-committally. 'Have you got a new man on the scene yet?' she asked, trying to change the subject.

'I'm working on it,' Julia answered, demurely sipping her drink, hoping her daughter wasn't sharp enough to pick up on her intentions and stop her from visiting. When Lynsey went into the bathroom, Julia went over to the phone and dialled 1471. There had been a call earlier that evening and Lynsey had rung off fairly quickly, so Julia wasn't surprised to hear Jack's mobile number being spoken slowly by the mechanical voice at the other end. He'd given Julia his mobile number quite some time ago, for emergencies, but any time she called him, he was unavailable and he never got back to her.

She smiled and put the receiver down, slinking back to her seat just as Lynsey returned. *Once I close in on him, he won't stand a chance*, she thought confidently. She'd done it before and she could do it again, this time for good. However, she didn't want

Lynsey realising her ulterior motive, so she didn't mention him again. However, Lynsey almost bit her head off when she started asking about James Bolton, so she prattled on about John and Marcia getting married until Lynsey reminded her she had work in the morning, so she made her excuses and left early enough to pick up some more wine on her way home.

Lynsey saw Julia out of the flat, and knew with a sinking sense of resignation that her mother would be a regular visitor now, whether she liked it or not. They had never been close and Lynsey was only too well aware that she normally only got in touch with her when she wanted something. She hadn't quite figured out what that was as yet, but no doubt she would in time.

9

James's New Plan

The day dragged a little on the Friday of the Christmas night out. Just before lunchtime, a very petite, blonde teenage girl came into the office and stopped at reception for a moment to chat to Marcia. Then she walked breezily over to James's room. James lifted his head and saw the girl coming. He jumped up to go and meet her, smiling broadly. Lynsey heard him say, 'Hello, sweetheart!' before he closed the door. This must be his daughter, she realised. Her heart contracted at the tenderness in his eyes and she was aware that, in spite of how things were between them, she really wanted him to look at her that way and call her 'sweetheart', a situation that seemed very unlikely just then. She reminded herself again that he was not someone she should be thinking about at all, especially since he had started treating her so badly.

She was feeling rather excited when she left work. They were finishing early because of the dance and she was looking forward to it. She'd bought a new dress and could hardly wait to wear it. She wasn't much of a party person, generally speaking, but she hadn't been dancing for ages, so she was sure she would enjoy it. It felt like a long time since she'd had any fun.

In the car park, John winked at her as she was getting into her car and, after glancing around carefully, she laughed and blew him a kiss. As he drove away, she turned the key in the ignition and then jumped nervously as James suddenly appeared and bent down towards her window. She pressed the button to slide the window down and then wished she hadn't when she saw the scowl on his face.

'Just how many men do you need?' he snarled at her. 'Not content with ruining one marriage, you're trying to come between John and Marcia as well.'

She opened her mouth to protest and then thought better of it. What was the point? It must look to him as though she was flirting with John.

'I don't think you've got any room to talk about marriage, have you?' she threw back at him, hoping attack would be her best form of defence. 'You don't know the meaning of the word if your reputation's anything to go by!' she continued, getting into her stride. 'And I wish you'd make your mind up anyway. One minute you're calling me Goody Two-Shoes, the next I'm supposed to be running round with every man I know!'

He looked even angrier, but didn't reply, and she turned away and moved off, her good mood replaced by impotent rage. Obviously he didn't understand the situation, but that didn't give him the right to be so nasty and vicious with her. It was the first time he had attacked her like that in ages and she felt quite shaken by it. He had some nerve, speaking to her like that! She would ignore him tonight, she decided. In fact, maybe she would just ignore him all the time, and serve him right. *Who does he think he is anyway? He's no saint himself,* she fumed, blinking furiously to stop herself from crying.

When she got home she threw off her coat and shoes and poured a very large brandy to help settle her nerves, then she had a long soak in a scented bubble bath and took her time getting ready. She blow-dried her hair and drew it back from her face on one side with a pearl clasp. She slipped the midnight blue velvet dress over her head and then made her face up carefully. She was getting used to using heavier make-up now. After she had started darkening her hair, so that no one would see it was exactly the same colour as John's and Jack's, she'd started using more make-up to compensate for her pale complexion. For the first time, as she gazed at her reflection, she saw the resemblance to her mother, something she had never been aware of before. James's cutting remark that she had her mother's looks but not her personality came back into her mind.

Although she was pleased with her finished appearance, a frown still creased her brow. *I'm going to forget all about him*, she promised herself. *I'll just enjoy the dance and ignore him.*

* * *

As James headed home, his anger dissipated and he began to see the situation from a new angle. He was strongly attracted to Lynsey and he now admitted to himself that much of his anger was due to sheer frustration, and also impatience with his own weakness. She was ruining his friends' lives, and it puzzled him that neither of them seemed able to see that she was using them. Even more puzzling was the fact that *he* still wanted her although he knew what she was up to with them, but that was *his* problem. He was convinced that Jack and John were deluding themselves and that if they knew what she was really like they'd run a mile.

As these scattered thoughts merged together he began to see a way forward, a strategy that would both give him a release from his frustration and make sure John and Jack stopped having anything to do with her. All at once, it seemed obvious what he should do. He was going to seduce her! *Shouldn't be too difficult*, he thought bitterly, *she obviously likes plenty of notches on her bedpost.* Then he'd make sure Jack and John knew all about it. Suddenly, he had a flashback to the look on her face when they'd rowed earlier and he realised how badly he'd mishandled the situation. How could he make a move on her now when he'd alienated her as much as he had? She was furious with him.

He also realised that, ironically, the person best equipped to give him advice was Lynsey herself! He turned this over in his mind for a while. His cause seemed quite hopeless until he remembered that she was good at helping people to sort out difficult situations in their lives. *What would she suggest if I was one of the guys asking her for advice?* he wondered. The answer was simple – he should use the bad blood between them as leverage to draw her in. And to be believable he would have to include a lot of truth in his explanations and apologies to her. He would have to be prepared to eat some humble pie and confess his feelings of attraction and frustration! It was the only way it would work. She'd never be taken in otherwise; she certainly wasn't stupid and nobody could ever accuse her of being insensitive.

Pleased with his new plan, and convinced it would work, he felt much happier as he drove through the streets of Hamilton and arrived at the large, rambling house he shared with his wife. He noticed that her car wasn't there, so put his car in the garage. He went round to the back door, as he always did, and went inside. The back of the house had been his living space for some time and he knew Gina wouldn't disturb him when she came in. While Lisa was growing up they'd merely had separate bedrooms, but now they lived completely separate lives under the same roof. He poured himself a larger whisky than usual because he wouldn't be driving that night and also to help steady his growing excitement. He didn't want to appear tense or she'd smell a rat. He tried not to think about rats, reminding himself, as he showered and changed, that he was doing this to help his friends and also to teach *her* that there was a price to be paid if she was going to continue wrecking other people's relationships.

10

The Dance

Lynsey heard a knock at her door and went to let John and Marcia in. As Forrest & Bolton was a small company, they were sharing the venue with two other office parties. She always hated walking into a large, busy place by herself, so they were all going to the hotel together. John looked tall, slim and handsome, and even though Marcia had a bit of a tummy now, she looked stunning in a pale gold halter-neck dress. The morning sickness was easing up and happiness was lending her skin as much of a glow as the dress.

'You look lovely, Marcia,' Lynsey said.

'I was just going to say that to you,' Marcia answered. She smiled warmly at Lynsey in the way she had when she'd first met her, and Lynsey was glad that Marcia knew their secret. Now they would always be friends. She had made the decision to break her promise to Jack and, with hindsight, Lynsey was sure she had done the right thing.

For a moment she wondered if she should do the same thing regarding James. What if she put him straight on a few things – would he get off her case and realise she wasn't the scheming manipulator he obviously thought she was? She pictured his face, filled with anger and contempt for her, and she realised that it would probably take more than that to get through to him. There was obviously something else going on beneath the surface. It was a lost cause and there was no point in pretending otherwise. Her heart felt heavy inside her chest as she finally admitted to herself the reason for that. She wasn't just infatuated, as she had tried so hard to convince herself she was. The truth was, she was emotionally involved with him. She swallowed her growing despair, smiled brightly at John and Marcia and led the way out of the door. They all piled into the waiting cab and headed off to the dance.

Later that evening, with the dance in full swing, Lynsey had had a few more drinks and lots of dances and although she was still annoyed at James, she reminded herself that he was convinced he had good reason to be annoyed with her, given his suspicions, and her anger had softened a little. It was almost impossible to ignore him as she'd intended doing. He looked very attractive in his evening suit and was dancing and smiling and being nice to everyone.

Towards the end of the evening, the band played a slow dance, announced as Ladies' Choice, and she asked John to dance with her. She watched as Marcia went over to James and moved onto the floor with him. He kept looking over at her and John and she was really surprised when he actually smiled at her! She smiled back tentatively. *He can't have just forgotten about this afternoon, just like that*, she thought. But maybe they'd had to hit rock bottom to bounce back up again. *Maybe everything will be all right now*, she tried to tell herself. It was Christmas, after all, the season of goodwill.

In the middle of the dance, when James and Marcia passed by them, Lynsey was amazed when James tapped John on the shoulder and asked him if he would like to swap partners! John looked enquiringly at Lynsey, and when she nodded he let her go and happily swept Marcia into the centre of the dance floor. Lynsey went into James's arms like the proverbial lamb to the slaughter. She was still angry with him but also angry with herself for still wanting him even though he'd been horrible to her. She just wanted things to be right between them. At that moment, although they were surrounded by people, she felt as though they were alone on the dance floor, alone in the world – together. But there was no way she was going to let him know that, especially after the way he'd spoken to her earlier that day. She kept her face averted so he wouldn't see how emotional she was feeling.

'Lynsey,' he said urgently, 'I need to apologise to you for this afternoon. I was well out of order. I don't know what got into me. I hope you can forgive me.'

She didn't answer. She wasn't sure if he was serious or not.

He bent his head towards her and she tensed, expecting a sarcastic comment to follow the apology, but instead he smiled into her eyes and told her how lovely she looked. Her eyes narrowed suspiciously.

'Why are you being so nice to me all of a sudden?' she asked warily.

'Maybe I've always wanted to be nice to you,' he said lightly, and she was stunned to realise he was actually flirting with her!

'Oh, then why haven't you?' she demanded.

'You're always making out that there's a lot of things I don't understand about you, Lynsey, but maybe there's a few things you don't understand about me, either.'

'I'd say that's a safe bet,' she said softly.

'Well, how about we go somewhere a bit quieter where we can talk?'

She looked unsure and said, 'Won't your wife be waiting for you?'

'No,' was all he said.

'Well, OK – where do you want to go then? It's getting quite late.'

'Hmm … a club's too noisy, it's too cold to go for a walk and I haven't got the car. We could take a taxi to your flat.'

She wasn't too happy about that, given his past antagonism, but there really wasn't any alternative if they were going to talk privately.

'Well … I'd have to let John and Marcia know. We were supposed to be going home together.' She watched his face to see if that would make him back off.

'Of course,' he said straight away, trying not to give himself away by looking too pleased.

They walked over to John and Marcia, who were obviously quite surprised when James said he was going to take Lynsey home. John frowned and looked at Lynsey enquiringly.

'It's okay, John. We've got a lot of talking to do, and now's as good a time as any,' she told him reassuringly.

John still looked uncertain. 'Well, you know where I am if you need me, Lynsey,' he told her, and she nodded.

'You *will* look after her?' John asked, turning to James.

'Oh I will, don't you worry.' James couldn't keep from smiling now.

'*He's* in a good mood tonight, isn't he?' John remarked to Marcia.

'Mm. Must be the Christmas spirit!' she responded as they faced each other for the last dance.

* * *

Lynsey felt light-hearted as they left the cab and skipped up the stairs to her flat together. The unpleasantness between them seemed to be over and they were going to call a truce, she was sure. Her heart was racing and her hand shook a little as she turned the key in the lock. *What am I nervous about?* she wondered. *We're only going to talk.*

She took off her fluffy white fun-fur coat and asked James if he would like to take off his evening jacket.

'Yes, I think I will, if you don't mind,' he said politely. She hung them up next to each other.

'Would you like a drink, James?' she offered, walking over to the cabinet against the wall.

'Yes, please,' he said, smiling, 'although I don't suppose you've any whisky?'

'I do have whisky, actually. I always keep some for Jack.' She stopped speaking and turned her head to look at him. The smile was frozen on his face.

He drew in a soft breath. 'Fine,' he said, and she relaxed again.

He sat down on the chair facing the settee and she handed him the glass of whisky. They looked at each other as their fingers connected. She felt flustered and put down her own glass to go and fiddle with the music centre. She chose a Dean Martin CD, as they both needed to relax a little, and sat down on the settee facing James. He raised his eyebrows in surprise and wondered if she'd chosen the music to suit him. *After all, she's used to pleasing different age groups, isn't she?* he reminded himself. The bitterness of the thought squashed the stirrings of discomfort he was beginning to feel with his plan of action. He had to stay focused and just go for it.

'Nice place,' he commented non-committally.

'Thanks,' she answered, then added, 'Jim, I know you must be wondering—'

'Let's cut to the chase, shall we?' he interrupted, adding innocently, 'I don't want to keep you up all night.'

Her eyes widened a little, but she sipped her drink and said nothing. The ball was in his court. He spoke quietly and quickly.

'First of all, I need to apologise again for this afternoon.' He put a hand up to stop her interrupting. 'And for all the other times I've been out of order with you.' She stayed silent, waiting for his explanation.

He took a deep breath, finished his drink, and laid down his glass. 'I know an apology isn't enough – you deserve a proper explanation. The only way I can explain it to you is that I was being totally unfair and taking everything out on you.'

She was puzzled but didn't speak, as it was obvious that he hadn't finished.

'I … there's been a lot of stuff happening at home with Gina, and my marriage is as good as over.'

Her head came up swiftly and she looked relieved. He knew he was making progress with her.

'She's really been giving me a hard time and all the bad feelings I've kept inside for so long just seemed to come out all at once. I was mad as hell with her and you got the brunt of it.' He stopped for a second and then began again. 'I know what you're thinking – why take it out on you? Well, I think it was because I was mad at you anyway, because of Jack. We go back a long way, you know, not just Jack but May as well.'

She stood up and went over to pour them each another drink. She had a feeling they would need it.

'Jim—' she began.

'No, please don't stop me. If I don't say this now I never will.' He downed half of his drink in one go.

'I've behaved really badly towards you because … because I was frustrated.' He swallowed nervously. He wasn't sure how she would react to this. He had a hunch that she was attracted to him, because he'd sometimes caught her looking at him and then quickly looking away again, but he wasn't sure.

'What I'm trying to say is – I was jealous.' He stopped and looked away from her. She blinked and stared at him and a long sigh escaped her. She came over to the settee and sat down right beside him.

'You know, there's really no need to feel that way. There's nothing to be jealous of.'

He still didn't look at her.

'I can't explain about Jack right now, but I will soon,' she promised. 'All I can say is that things aren't always the way they look.'

No, but they usually are, he thought cynically. He stood up and moved away.

'What difference does it make – I've blown it now anyway, haven't I? I've been such a sod I haven't got a chance with you now – if I ever did in the first place.'

He looked at the carpet, his hands in his pockets, his shoulders down, trying to keep his face straight. He hadn't expected this to be so easy or to feel so good. Pretending to be upset wouldn't have worked; she'd have seen straight through him. Right now he didn't want to be anywhere else in the world. He was standing on a mountaintop. He was king, he was in control. He wasn't faking his emotional state – he just wasn't being honest about the cause. Lynsey was doing exactly what he wanted her to do – misconstruing his state of nervous tension.

He looked at her as she touched his arm gently and turned him to face her. He was trembling a little. Whatever else she was, she was a genuinely compassionate person and his scruples were beginning to bother him again. But he hadn't forgotten why he was here and if he put it off he wouldn't get another chance like this. Two birds with one stone!

She was a lovely young woman and everything else left his mind as she put her arms around him and held him close. Her perfume was subtle and sexy and his sigh of appreciation wasn't faked either. He stroked her hair gently and tilted her face up towards him. He tried to speak, but his mouth had other ideas and he found himself kissing her forehead, her temple, her cheek. Then their lips met in a kiss that both of them had wanted for so long that it was never going to be enough for either of them. They started undressing each other, neither of them having any agenda at that moment other than satisfying their mutual passion.

11

The Morning After

When Lynsey awoke the next morning she smiled and sighed as she opened her eyes and saw her blue dress, lying in a heap on the floor. Her little black cami was wrapped around her waist. She moved to get up and James pulled her closer. His arm lay heavily over her and she couldn't move. She wouldn't have minded at all if her bladder weren't full to bursting. *Shouldn't have had all that wine, I suppose*, she thought languorously. It didn't really matter. Nothing seemed to matter any more. She felt as if nothing would ever bother her again. It was just as well she didn't know how wrong she was.

'Let me up, Jim, I need to go,' she said, a smile in her voice.

'Go where?' he teased her.

'There'll be a very nasty accident in a moment if you keep me here,' she warned.

'OK, off you go, on condition you come straight back.'

'Where else would I go?' she pointed out.

'Just be quick, that's all,' he explained.

'Why – will you miss me?' she asked hopefully.

'No, I mean I need to go myself!' he said, laughing, as if he hadn't a care in the world. He watched her go. She felt shy in the morning light and pulled her gown around her as soon as she was out of the bed.

No prancing around naked for this girl, he thought, *she's good at doing the coy bit. Pity it's wasted on me.*

In the bathroom mirror she looked at her reflection. *This is what happiness looks like*, she reflected as she washed her hands. She'd had sex quite a few times in her life, but this was the first time she'd ever felt that she had made love. When she came back she threw herself into the bed, intending to grab hold of him and keep him back as he had done with her, but he slipped out of her reach, laughing again, and ran into the bathroom.

When he came back he reached for her and she was happy to snuggle into him, but when he began to caress her she drew back from him.

'I'm not much of a morning person, I'm afraid,' she said apologetically. 'Shall I make us some breakfast?'

'Not yet,' he answered. He looked down at her and thought, *If it wasn't for that hair, she'd be just perfect.* Her make up had worn off during the night and he liked her much better like that.

She started to speak again but he put his fingers on her lips to stop her. Last night the sex had been really good but a bit rushed because they were so eager, and he was aware that it had ended too soon for her. He wasn't going to leave things like this. And anyway, Jack wasn't likely to arrive for another hour or so.

He began to stroke and caress her very gently but extremely thoroughly. She was convinced there wasn't an inch of her left untouched. Gradually, she became so aroused that she was much more responsive and passionate than she usually was. He entered her and then he lay still and she looked up at him in surprise. He laid his hands on either side of her face and looked into her eyes. They intrigued him. As soon as he'd met her, he'd felt there was something strangely familiar about them. He kissed her mouth, sliding his tongue along hers sensuously, and their bodies began to move together. Her response was immediate and her release was swiftly followed by his. She was very glad they had made love again. They lay together during the afterglow and held each other close for a long time.

* * *

Some time later, James emerged from the shower and went into the little kitchen. He looked fresh and neat, except for his shirt, which he had left hanging outside his trousers. Lynsey was moving around whisking up scrambled eggs, frying bacon and singing happily to herself, but there was no smile on *his* face now. He still had a job to do and he was beginning to worry that Jack wasn't going to show up after all. Simply telling Jack about it wouldn't be the same – it would be so much more effective for him to see them together.

As though this thought had actually summoned him up, the doorbell rang. James squared his shoulders and called out, 'I'll get it!'

He opened the door, tucking his shirt casually into his trousers as he did so. He didn't even have to bother feigning surprise. Jack was so taken aback he was speechless and wouldn't have noticed the expression on James's face in any case. He just stood there and stared.

'Hi there, Jack,' James said chattily. 'Lynsey, it's Jack!' he called over his shoulder as if this were an everyday occurrence.

Lynsey appeared behind him, in her towelling robe, munching a piece of toast, and Jack took a couple of steps back. *No misconstruing this set-up*, he thought.

'I'll … catch you later,' he muttered.

'Jack, wait!' Lynsey called after him, but he was gone.

'Oh well,' she said, sighing. 'I'll speak to him later. I don't suppose it matters but I didn't really want him to find out about us like that.'

'No? Well I did,' James said pointedly as he reached for his jacket.

It was a moment before Lynsey took in what he was saying. 'What do you mean, James?' she asked, confused. 'What are you doing, aren't you staying for breakfast?'

'I've had everything I came for,' he said, slowly and meaningfully, and Lynsey gasped as if he had hit her. She didn't want to believe what she was hearing. She stared at him, trying to understand.

'Jim, what's going on? Why are you being like this? Did Jack say something to you?'

'Hardly!' was all he said.

He desperately wanted to get away now, so that he wouldn't have to look at her pale, shocked face. He'd done what he'd set out to do and he turned and bolted out of the door, closing it noisily behind him.

She stood still for some minutes, until the smoke alarm went off, galvanising her to run to the hob and switch off the heat. Then she opened all the windows and went to get dressed, all the while trying to understand what had just happened and why. Thinking back to their conversation at the door, it didn't take her long to figure out that he had set her up, but she couldn't even begin to understand why.

While she tried to figure things out, she began to clear up her things from the night before, moving slowly, automatically. When she lifted her dress from the floor, she threw it into the back of the wardrobe. It would need dry cleaning. *Why bother, I'll never want to wear it again*, she thought miserably, *not now*. She put her face in her hands. The tears came slowly at first, building to anguished sobbing as the events of the previous night and that morning played over and over in her head and she realised what a fool she'd been. After all the times he'd been awful to her, she had believed him and trusted him. Was she really so naïve and gullible? She'd been taken in and used in the worst possible way. Before Jack had arrived, she'd been planning to have a talk with James over breakfast, to make sure he knew she valued fidelity above all else and wouldn't normally go with a married man at all. His good opinion had been important to her, and she'd wanted him to understand that, through Jack, she'd already known that his marriage to Gina was non-existent. She'd felt sure they would be good together and could have a promising relationship, and all the time he'd been planning to do this to her!

Eventually she stopped crying and she also stopped trying to understand his values and motivations. Whatever his reasons were, she felt so horribly humiliated she was sure she would *never* forgive him.

12

Living a Lie

That morning, because she was so distraught, Lynsey considered ringing her mother and asking if she could come another time. She didn't think she'd be able to hold herself together in front of anyone, but as the day wore on, a deep, burning anger towards James Bolton gradually began to drown out the misery she had felt before, and she found she was actually looking forward to having Julia staying with her. Maybe some simple, uncomplicated company was just what she needed. It would help her to stop dwelling on what had happened. So she spent the morning getting some shopping in, tidying the flat and changing the sheets on the beds. She wrapped up the silk scarf she had bought her mother for Christmas so that she wouldn't see it lying around, and placed it under her little silver Christmas tree. As she did so, she reminded herself that she should ring Jack and let him know Julia was staying with her, in case he decided to drop in unexpectedly. She knew he tried to avoid meeting up with Julia whenever possible. However, when she tried to reach him, there was no answer, and after a couple of attempts, she gave up and left a message on his mobile.

* * *

Julia arrived, mid-afternoon, in a cloud of smoke and Christian Dior. Lynsey gave her a quick hug and went over to open the window.

'I thought John might be here,' Julia said chattily as she opened a bottle of Chardonnay with the ease that comes from a great deal of practice.

'He was at the dance last night,' Lynsey told her. 'I think he'll be quite busy with wedding preparations this weekend, though. Where shall we go tonight? Is there anything you want to do?'

'Maybe we'll just stay here and watch a video,' Julia suggested, 'but we'll need more wine – we don't want to be running out again, do we?'

Lynsey raised her eyebrows at the idea of Julia sitting in quietly on a Saturday evening. 'Well, I'll go and get some more, later on,' she promised, quite happy to put her feet up and relax for a while.

'I expect I'll be meeting Marcia's family soon,' Julia said casually, then hesitated a little. 'And Jack will be, too. They'll be wanting to meet him as well, won't they?'

'Mother, they can't meet Jack just now, you know that,' Lynsey said, exasperated.

'I don't see why not.'

'Because Jack still hasn't told May about – things.'

'You're kidding!' Julia gasped. She sounded shocked, but in reality she had suspected this was the case. She hadn't been able to question Lynsey or John about it directly because they would have wondered why she was interested after all this time. This was going to be easier than she'd thought. Lynsey had just handed Jack to her on a plate – and she wouldn't even have to hang around for ages waiting for him to appear!

'Jack *is* going to tell her soon, you know,' Lynsey said defensively. 'He has to, really, now that John's engaged.'

'Yes,' said Julia, her brain beginning to work overtime, 'I'm sure he will.' *If he was ever going to tell her he'd have done it by now*, was what she was really thinking.

* * *

Jack was sitting at the dinner table looking at his wife and thinking exactly the same thing.

I'll tell her this week, he promised himself. *But I won't wait till the end of the week, like I did last time. I'll just enjoy this lovely peaceful weekend at home with her and then I'll come home from work on Monday evening and I'll do it. I will! I've made up my mind to do it now. I have to. That way we'll have made up again by next week and Christmas won't be spoiled.*

* * *

When Monday came Jack was still resolute. Time to bite the bullet and just get on with it. He'd had his 'last weekend', as he thought of it, with May. He was ready for it now. He had kept himself really busy all day so that he wouldn't have a chance to get worked up about it. Lynsey's message to him on Saturday morning about Julia visiting her at the flat had really unnerved him and he realised it was now or never.

At 5 o'clock, he looked through his office window at Lynsey and signalled for her to wait behind. When the rest of the staff had gone, she went into his room.

'I'm going to speak to May tonight, Lynsey,' he told her. 'No backing out this time.'

She didn't say anything, but didn't look too convinced.

'I hope it goes okay then, Jack, I really do.'

'I know you think I won't do it, because I haven't been able to before, but it's different now. I'm sure I can do it at last.'

'So, what's different now?'

'It's just got to the stage where there's no putting it off any longer. And there's John's engagement. It has to come out now, one way or another, and I want to be the one to tell her. I think that will make a big difference.'

Lynsey smiled encouragingly and tried to ignore the sinking feeling in her stomach.

'I'm sure it will, Jack, I'm sure it will,' she told him, but he thought she seemed less than convinced and he didn't really blame her.

Unusually for him, Jack drove at a steady pace all the way home, trying to contain his nervous excitement. This was it. Whatever happened, after today he would be free of this burden. He was really pleased because, for once, it looked as if his nerves weren't going to let him down. He remembered that day, all those years ago, when May had told him she was sorry for being distant with him and that she wanted things to get back to normal between them again. They'd made love passionately and he had known that he couldn't tell her what had happened with Julia, every instinct telling him that he'd lose her for ever if he did, and he couldn't bear the thought of that. But they'd been together for a long time now, so surely it wouldn't have such a drastic effect on her now as it would have had all that time ago?

As he approached the house, he noticed there was another car in the driveway, one he didn't recognise, parked very near the door. He drew in behind it and walked up the steep driveway, and he was amazed at how calm he felt. But he felt strangely flat, too, which couldn't be normal, he thought, given the situation. He put his hand out to open the door and it opened up unexpectedly, before he touched it. He jumped back as Julia Robson emerged, and she certainly didn't look as shocked to see him as he was to see her. She gave him a forced little smile.

'Well, Jack, it's been a long time, hasn't it?' she said, a little breathlessly. She swallowed, and even in the dark he could see that her face was unusually flushed. He stared at her in horror. He stuttered, trying to ask her what she was doing here, but every nerve in his body told him he already knew. He was shaking his head. All he could say was 'no', over and over. He couldn't take it in, it wasn't meant to happen like this. *He* was going to do it, right now. Him, not Julia. God, not Julia. He turned and dashed into the house, along the hallway and into the softly-lit lounge. May was sitting very still, staring into space, her fair head bent and her soft blue eyes glazed over with pain and disbelief. A lump rose in his throat. There were so many things he wanted to say, but all he managed to do was whisper hoarsely 'May…'

He stood very still and held his breath. Eventually she looked at him and blinked.

'Julia was here,' she said shakily. 'Julia Smith.'

Not knowing exactly what Julia had said to her, Jack went over and sat down next to her. He touched her shoulder and started to speak. 'May, I – it—'

'It was all a lie,' she said, pathetically, 'all a lie.'

'No' he said, in an anguished whisper. 'No. I don't know what she said to you but you have to believe me—'

'Believe you, Jack? Oh yes, I've always believed you, haven't I? What a fool. A stupid, silly fool.'

'No, he said, 'no.' His heart was hammering now, he was sweating and his mouth had gone very dry. All the words he'd rehearsed in his head earlier, to explain things to her, had deserted him.

'May, what happened with Julia was a mistake, the worst mistake of my life. I—'

'Yes', she said bitterly, 'the worst mistake of my life, too.'

He cringed. 'May, it wasn't an affair. It only happened once – John and Lynsey are twins. You know how things were between us at that time, just after we found out there wouldn't be any children. You didn't want me near you – '

'Oh, so it was my fault, is that what you're saying?'

'Of course not – I didn't mean that.'

'How could you, Jack? How could you?'

'I know that I was totally to blame. I was weak and stupid. It was a dreadful mistake. I've thought about it every day of my life since. I'd give anything not to have hurt you like this.'

'A bit late for regrets now!'

He started to speak, but stopped again. How could he tell her he'd never regretted it because if he hadn't gone with Julia he wouldn't have had the children?

May spoke again, in a voice dry and hoarse with pain. 'I'm not talking about you going with Julia, Jack. I'm talking about John and

Lynsey. How could you? How could you have two children and not even tell me – how could you do that?' She looked at him as if he were a stranger to her. 'I don't even know you, I don't know who you are. Our whole life is a lie, nothing but a lie. All of it.'

'No, May, no, you're wrong. You couldn't be more wrong. I love you. Please don't—' he pleaded.

'Don't what? Don't hate you? I don't hate you, Jack. How could I – I don't even know you.'

'May—'

'Get out, Jack. Get out.' Her voice rose and she stood up. 'Get out! Get …out!' she shouted at him. He was standing now, too.

'I understand,' he said carefully. 'I know you need time to take all this in.' Her eyes flared and her breath hissed out of her mouth slowly.

'I'll come back later and we can talk then,' he said, moving to the door and turning to look at her sadly.

'Go!' she yelled, as though she couldn't bear to look at him for a moment longer.

He left.

13

Aftermath

Lynsey moved quickly towards her front door to answer the insistent knocking. She knew before she got there that it was Jack. She drew back the bolt and he almost fell into the hallway when the door opened.

'Jack, what on earth—?' she began, but she stopped speaking when she saw his face.

'She threw me out,' he told her in a dazed voice. 'Lynsey, she threw me out. What am I going to do?'

'Come and sit down,' she said, taking his arm and leading him into the lounge. She poured him a large whisky and put it into his hand. He looked at it blankly and she poured herself a drink, too. She had a feeling she was going to need it. She took a couple of sips of her wine and looked at her father, wanting to help but knowing he was too shocked to be easily comforted.

'She took it badly, then?'

He nodded.

'Well, you must have known it would be a terrible shock to her. What did you expect?' she asked, trying not to sound harsh, but a little puzzled as to why he was so surprised.

'Your bloody mother,' he ground out. He banged his glass

down on the coffee table and leaned towards Lynsey, glaring at her. 'It's down to her, all of it. I'll never forgive her. When I get my hands on her—'

'What do you mean, Dad? You haven't even seen her for years.'

Lynsey looked at him and then realisation began to dawn. 'Oh no,' she groaned.

'Oh yes, Lynsey. She got there before me, didn't she?' Tears came into his eyes and he hung his head. 'It should have been me. I should have told her. It wouldn't have been so bad if I'd told her myself.'

Still trying to take in the enormity of what her mother had done, and beginning to realise her motivation for doing it, Lynsey tried to calm him as best she could, feeling as if she was falling apart inside herself. This had been a long time coming and emotions were running high. She had thought she would be mentally prepared for the turmoil the revelations would bring, but she was only now becoming aware that it was going to affect all of their lives permanently. What Julia had done couldn't be undone and all they could do was try to minimise the damage and salvage what they could. Right now Lynsey was too preoccupied with trying to ease Jack's distress to feel any real anger towards Julia, but that would come, and when it did, Julia would be sorry. She would live to regret the havoc she had so recklessly caused. After all the time they had spent waiting for Jack to bring things to a head himself, it had been cruel of her to do this to him.

Lynsey thought of all the things she'd had to endure because of Jack's secret. All those long years full of waiting. She and John had waited many times for Jack to come and see them. Sometimes he had made it, but often they simply got a phone call – they were no strangers to disappointment. Then, as adults, waiting to be acknowledged as his children, they had felt as though they had a guilty secret themselves, although they had done nothing wrong. She had moved to Lanarkshire at her father's request, to help him bring things to a head and face up to telling May, but Lynsey had even had to change her appearance to come here, as she and John were twins with very similar colouring and Jack was anxious that no one would make the connection before he was ready. Also, she'd had to use heavier make-up to offset the darker hair, and so she'd had to put up with James Bolton making her life a misery because she looked like a tart!

Lynsey had expected a violent reaction from May; she would have felt the same way herself in those circumstances. The truth had been bound to come out some time, but now she was beginning to wonder if Jack would be able to cope if May didn't forgive him. His wife meant everything to him, but right now, understandably, May wouldn't be seeing things quite like that.

Lynsey went through to the bedroom to make up the bed Julia had occupied two days before. The irony was not lost on her, and she vowed that a day of reckoning would come between her and Julia at some point. Not only had Julia betrayed Jack, she had used Lynsey in order to do so, and that wasn't easy to overlook.

* * *

In the morning, Lynsey was surprised when Jack was up and dressed before her. His burden had been lifted, for good or ill, and although he was still recovering from the emotional events of the previous night he was also, characteristically, full of positive energy. Over breakfast, she asked him what his plans were and he said he was going straight round to see May and sort things out with her.

'Dad, do you think that's a good idea?' she asked anxiously. 'I mean, she must still be gutted. I'd wait a little while if I were you – give her time to recover, then she'll be more likely to listen to you.'

He thought about this for a moment while he sipped his tea.

'Maybe you're right, love. Yes, I think maybe I'll wait till after work and then I'll go round and see her.'

Lynsey gave a sigh of relief and tried to eat something. Everything seemed tasteless to her these days. She took a little bite out of her toast and then put it down again. Later the two of them drove off to work at the same time and arrived together, talking in hushed tones as they walked into the office. A pair of dark brown, puzzled eyes watched from the other side of the room. She mentioned to Jack that it looked bad, their arriving together, but he just smiled and patted her head as she sat down.

As James walked towards them, Jack said, 'It doesn't matter now, love. Everyone will know soon enough.' Then he said, 'Good morning, Jim!' and went into his own room. James threw her a look, then turned on his heel and left the room. She was past caring, she told herself, and she was sick to death of his attitude. He was really getting on her nerves now.

In the middle of the afternoon, Lynsey was just putting a fax on Marcia's desk when she heard her putting a call through to James from a woman called Maisie. When she got back to her own desk she asked John who Maisie was and he smiled and said, 'Jim's girlfriend. They've been together now for … oh, about fifteen years.'

She turned away, trying not to let him see her reaction. She felt more than angry now. Jim had made a complete fool of her and she had let him. She had no time for men who thought it was smart to keep several different women on a string at the same time and she also, if she was honest with herself, felt totally crushed that she meant so little to him. Her jaw tightened as she promised herself that she would never be taken in by him again.

About half an hour later, Nick was sitting on her desk chatting her up, and she was more receptive to him than normal, noticing out of the corner of her eye that James was watching them.

'We could go for a drink after work, if you like,' she suggested.

His brows shot up in surprise. 'You bet I like!' he answered, smiling broadly.

'I'll see you later then,' she answered, turning back to her work.

* * *

Towards the end of the day, Jack lifted the phone and dialled his home number. It rang for a long time before May answered.

'May,' he said, relieved that she had answered at last, 'are you feeling better today?'

Silence.

'May—'

'I'm not sick, Jack,' she answered slowly, as though she were speaking to someone who was slow-witted.

His stomach tightened into a knot.

'I'm coming home straight from work and we can have a good long talk,' he said reassuringly, his innate self-confidence coming to his rescue.

'The hell we can,' she hissed.

'But May—'

The line went dead and he stood holding the receiver for a moment before pressing the re-dial button. It was engaged. *She's taken it off the hook*, he thought, frustration and fear rising ominously inside him.

* * *

When everyone except Jack and James had left to go home, Lynsey waited until she saw James heading over towards the coat cupboard, then she got up and went into Jack's room, leaving the door open so that James wouldn't think there was anything going on between them. *He* might have a questionable moral code, but she didn't want anyone thinking *she* did, including him. James put his jacket on and walked over to the outside door. Then he looked back at the pair of them whispering together, and the elation and anticipation he'd felt all day came to a head. They could pretend to everyone else that everything was fine, but he knew better! It seemed strange to him that they hadn't had this out with each other on the Saturday night or the Sunday, but possibly Jack hadn't been able to get away from May.

They were about to have a major row and he doubted if they'd still be together afterwards. This was *his* doing and he wanted to savour the moment. *I'd like to be a fly on that wall*, he thought as he put his hand out to push the swing door. *Well, why not?* They had left the room door open, but had their backs to him, and they thought everyone had gone home. He turned round, slipped stealthily past the closed blinds of Jack's room and into his own, and stood behind the open door like a child waiting for the curtain to go up on a Christmas Panto.

In his own room, Jack gave Lynsey a direct, questioning look. She knew what was coming.

'Lynsey, about Saturday,' he began. He had been aware of her quiet misery all day and of James's smugness; he had to say something to her.

'James Bolton, Lynsey, a married man. You of all people. I still can't believe it. What were you thinking?'

There's nothing she can say to get out of this! thought James, holding his breath.

'I know. I don't even want to talk about it, Jack. I've been so stupid. But trust me, it won't ever be happening again,' she said grimly.

James exhaled, frowning. This wasn't right. Their conversation wasn't going the way it should do at all. He had expected a major confrontation: crying, pleading, remonstrating. *And what did Jack mean by 'going with a married man'? What was Jack if he wasn't a married man, for heaven sake!*

'It's so embarrassing, Lynsey,' Jack was saying now. He's my friend, and we all have to work together. It's going to be very awkward now.'

How can he be so cold-blooded? James wondered, becoming even more puzzled.

'I know,' Lynsey replied, sighing heavily. 'Do you think I should leave?'

'No, no, don't do that. Why should you, anyway? Let things settle down and we'll see how it goes. I'm sorry, love, I'm not being much help, am I? I'm so selfish. All I can think about is May right now.'

James was really perplexed now. This just wasn't making sense at all. *What is he made of? Is he just going to accept it and carry on as if nothing's happened?*

'I know, I know,' Lynsey said soothingly. 'But *you* aren't being selfish, *I* am. You don't need all this other aggravation when you've got so much on your plate with May.'

'James's got quite a reputation with the ladies. I take it you weren't disappointed!' Jack said mischievously.

'Dad!' Lynsey gasped, blushing. 'I'm not talking to you about that kind of stuff!'

James was as still as a mouse now, straining his ears to make sure he wasn't imagining things. *Am I going mad?* he thought. *She called him Dad! Or did she? Maybe she said Jack and it just sounded like Dad.* But their words hadn't been muffled, he could hear them quite clearly. He leaned against the wall for support and listened intently, his heart beginning to thump heavily.

'I do like it when you call me Dad,' said Jack. 'I know now's not the time to go public, but very soon everyone will know. A pity it's come a bit late for John, but he and Marcia seem to have survived. John's going to have in-laws and they're going to want to know his family history. He paused. 'He told her, didn't he?'

'We both did. Had to, really. Don't worry, Dad, it'll all work out in the end,' she said soothingly. They stopped speaking. James could picture them giving each other a hug, a father and daughter comforting each other, just as they'd done in Jack's car the day he'd followed them. In such a short space of time, like the turn of a kaleidoscope, the picture had changed completely. He was sweating now and he had one hand over his mouth for fear that he would make a noise and give himself away. He heard them walking across the office and going out through the main door, locking it behind them, and then he groaned and went over to his desk to sit down. He opened the desk drawer and took out the glass and whisky bottle he kept there. He poured out a little and swallowed it in one go.

'Jesus,' he said out loud, 'tell me this isn't happening.'

14

Breaking Point

James sat at his desk for some time, trying to steady himself and collect his thoughts. His initial surge of heartfelt relief that Jack and Lynsey weren't involved with each other was strong but short-lived. *How many times did she tell me I didn't know the facts, that it wasn't the way it looked?* He thought back and cringed inside as he remembered the things he had said to her, the way he had treated her. And then his mind went to the night they had spent together.

'*Things aren't always the way they look*,' she'd said to him when he'd mentioned Jack. He groaned as he recalled the expression on her face when he'd left her standing in the flat the next morning. A few other things had also begun to fall into place. From what he'd just overheard, it didn't take a genius to work out that John was Jack's son and Lynsey's brother!

And that wasn't the worst of it – he'd alienated John, too. That morning he'd stood and waited, smiling, for John to remark that he looked very pleased with himself.

'I presume you had a good weekend, Jim. Blonde or brunette?' he'd asked, momentarily forgetting that James had taken Lynsey home from the dance. James had looked straight at him and said, 'Why don't you ask Lynsey?' and had walked away, leaving John looking shocked and disbelieving. He had obviously given John the impression that he thought very little of Lynsey. And, to make matters worse, he'd always contrived to give people the impression that he had little respect for women generally. It had been his way of coping with the humiliation of Gina's attitude towards him.

James bent forward onto the desk with his hands covering his face, trying to escape from the inevitable onslaught of regret and self-recrimination, but there was no hiding place. After a time he looked up. It was just as well he had his own key for the office. He had to get home and think this through properly. No couple of drinks for him tonight. Tonight he was going to get very, very drunk.

* * *

When he arrived home he let himself in through the back door and went straight over to the cabinet where he kept his whisky. Once the alcohol had softened his feelings a little, he settled down into his favourite armchair and tried to assess the situation. He didn't like the results. His behaviour had been unacceptable. Even if his suspicions about Lynsey had been right, setting her up like that had been a spiteful thing to do. His motives hadn't been altruistic, as he'd tried to convince himself they were. He could admit now that he'd acted out of jealousy and spite, and he was convinced that Lynsey was unlikely ever to forgive him. He'd broken his own first rule: *Never assume anything. Get your facts straight and then decide what to do.* He'd always given this very good advice to his younger colleagues when he was training them to handle clients and property deals. His other favourite piece of advice was never to make the same mistake twice. Well, he wouldn't make this mistake twice. He wouldn't get the chance, if he knew anything about Lynsey Robson.

He was still struggling to accept all the implications of the situation. It was difficult enough getting his head round the fact that Jack was Lynsey's father after believing them to be lovers, but John being Jack's son and Lynsey's brother – that blew his mind. This was going to take quite a bit of getting used to. He'd always thought Jack treated John like the son he'd never had. Now he knew he was the son he actually *did* have. James realised that he had betrayed his friends as well as Lynsey. He had believed the worst of them. Now they would believe the worst of him and he would deserve it! He closed his eyes in despair. How was he ever going to put things right? It wasn't just a mess, it was a disaster. What he had thought of, only that morning, as a triumph, he now knew was the worst thing he had ever done. And the hardest thing of all to accept was that he had only himself to blame.

* * *

Jack wasn't having a good evening either. He had been banging on the door of his and May's house for ages now and calling out her name, but she just wasn't answering. There was a light shining through the lounge window, but he was beginning to wonder if she had gone out and left the light on for security reasons. No, he was sure that she was in there, ignoring him.

'Please May,' he begged. 'Please can we talk? There's so much I want to say to you. This is pointless. We have to talk eventually. Please let me in,' he begged, thumping on the door yet again. Losing patience, he tried the door. It was locked. He pulled his key out of his pocket and put it in the lock. It stuck halfway in, refusing to turn in either direction, and he had to pull it back out again. His temper broke and he banged on the door again. It was no use, she wasn't going to answer and he realised that she'd had the locks changed! It seemed like he was just going to have to wait.

He gave up and strode back to his car. Within seconds he had sped off, on his way back to Uddingston. He was trying hard not to be angry at May because obviously that wasn't going to help him when she decided to speak to him again. He had to stay calm and she would eventually come round. She was bound to – then it would all be sorted out. He would grovel pathetically if he had to, if she would just give him a chance to!

May heard his car roaring off down the road. She looked out of the window to make sure he was gone. Then she went upstairs to continue packing his things. It was taking quite a while as he had a lot of gear. They both had. One of the bonuses of not having had any children to support, she'd used to think. *Not any more*, she thought bitterly. Nothing was the same any more. Nothing meant what it had before. All those years ... none of it had been real. And Jack had picked the wrong day to try and talk her round. Just when she'd thought she was recovering from the shock she'd had, she'd been dealt another blow.

She'd rung Jack's parents, who had been living abroad, in Provence, for a long time now. When she told them what Jack had done, they guiltily informed her that they already knew and that they had seen their grandchildren quite a few times over the years. She'd put the phone down in disgust. She felt betrayed all over again, but she didn't really blame his parents; she knew that Jack must have worked hard to get them to keep his secret. She could just picture him coaxing and cajoling them into believing that he would tell her in his own time, that they shouldn't interfere.

She began systematically bagging up everything that was his, and anything that belonged to them as a couple. She would carry on packing all night if she had to. There was no way he was getting back into what she now thought of as *her* house. She didn't need him any more, she told herself. She had her work at the Charity Shop and she would make an effort to make some new friends. She'd be just fine.

* * *

Jack had calmed down a little by the time he arrived at the flat. Thank goodness he'd bought the place when he had. He could have booked into a hotel, but then he would have felt as if he had left home for good, and there would have been no one to talk to about things. Lynsey was a godsend when you needed to talk. She was surprised to see him this early, but she had cooked dinner for him, so she had apparently been quite sure he would be back during the course of the evening! He gave a discouraged sigh as he poured himself a whisky and handed her a glass of wine.

'No joy?' she asked as she pottered about in the little kitchen, stirring a pot of Bolognese sauce and straining the spaghetti.

'Lynsey, she's keeping me out. She wouldn't come to the door. And I couldn't get in – she's had the locks changed!' he said, his anger rising to the surface again. She stopped what she was doing and stood in the kitchen doorway.

'She's what!' She didn't like what she was hearing at all.

'Obviously, she's still really mad at me and she's not going to take this lying down. Can't blame her, can you? I'll give it a few days, let her cool off and then I'll go over and sort it out. She can't ignore me forever. I can get into the house if I want to, you know. She hasn't any legal right to keep me out. It's just as much my house as hers. Don't worry, pet, I won't be here cramping your style for much longer!'

Lynsey turned away and started dishing the food out onto the plates, trying to stop her mind from racing ahead. It had come to this already, locks being changed and talk of legal rights. Jack was full of self-assurance, rather arrogantly assuming he could talk his wife round without too much trouble. That was his forté, after all, the art of persuasion. But Lynsey was gradually beginning to fear that May had suffered too deep a wound to bounce back after a little sweet-talk and protestations of love and devotion. She was very much afraid a little intervention was needed to smooth the way and get them back together again. They were made for each other and had always been a very loving couple, but this was a major breach in their relationship, not a minor setback, as her father seemed to think. It occurred to her that he knew this as well as she did and that he was kidding himself, probably because the alternative was unthinkable to him.

What would happen to him if May stayed adamant that she did not want to heal the breach, she wondered? She smiled half-heartedly at him as she served the meal and began to think of arguments she could use to persuade May to talk to him. *Maybe James Bolton was right after all,* she thought wryly, *she was doing her Little Miss Fix-It thing again!*

* * *

Lynsey soon found she couldn't fix it, however. The following day, May kept putting the phone down as soon as Lynsey began to speak. After quite a few attempts, she was getting a constant engaged tone and realised that May had no more intention of speaking to her than to her father. She felt frustrated and defeated and was trying hard to think of another way of approaching the situation. She mustn't panic, there must be something else she could try. She looked over to Jack's room and saw him having the same problem. She bit her lip. *It'll be all right,* she thought. *It has to be, for Jack's sake.*

At lunchtime she was writing a letter to May when James came over to her desk and waited a moment until she looked up at him. She had been vaguely aware that he hadn't been harassing her the way he usually did. He cleared his throat.

'I think we need to talk,' he said. 'Could we go somewhere after work? Tonight, if you're not too busy.'

'Whatever,' she said, shrugging, obviously preoccupied.

'Fine, I'll see you later then.'

'Right' she replied, getting on with her writing again.

* * *

At 5 o'clock, as they left the office together, she told Jack she would see him in a little while.

'There's chicken and salad in the fridge,' she said, and he glared darkly at James as they went their separate ways. Lynsey walked in silence to The Bar, with James walking pensively beside her.

When they got there he bought a beer and a Martini at the bar and they went over to the little corner table and sat down.

When they had both taken a couple of gulps of their drinks, he swallowed hard and started to speak nervously.

'Lynsey, I don't know where to start – I don't know how I can possibly apologise to you for what happened last week.'

'Neither do I,' she said quietly.

He hesitated, then tried again. 'Obviously I was under the impression—'

'That I was carrying on with Jack,' she finished. 'I told you a million times it wasn't what you thought.'

'I know, I know.' He drew one hand over his face in despair. 'I've gone over it again and again in my head and I think I just started off thinking badly of you and I just didn't believe anything you said after I'd seen the two of you together.'

'So you decided to sleep with me, then broadcast it to Jack and John so they'd see me for what I really am, is that it?' She looked at him steadily.

'Feel free to correct me if I'm wrong.' She spoke calmly, but there was an edge to her voice that belied the calmness.

'No, you're not wrong,' he admitted, sighing. 'I was the one who was wrong and what I did was—'

'Unforgivable.'

'Lynsey, if I could go back and change it I would …'

'Yes, so would I,' she answered bitterly, and stood up to go.

'Please, Lynsey, I want to make it up to you. I want us to start again—'

She looked at him as if he had grown two heads.

'Us? Are you out of your mind? If you think I would have anything to do with you now, you're crazy. And you had the nerve to ask me how many men *I* need!' she said angrily, shaking her head in disgust.

He looked confused. 'What do you mean?'

'What's Maisie then, scotch mist?'

'Me and Maisie are finished now, and it was only ever a casual relationship.'

'Casual – for fifteen years!' she challenged him.

'Neither Maisie nor I ever intended for things to be

permanent. We were two people with bad marriages. We stayed with our partners because of our children. The arrangement suited us both.'

'I'm very pleased for you,' she said sarcastically, at the same time admitting to herself that he hadn't really had any alternative, if things were as bad as they seemed to be with Gina. She realised that John had been stirring things again but at the same time, James had slept with her, Lynsey, when he already had not only a wife but a long-term girlfriend, too. Her normally sympathetic nature was swamped under all the anger she felt towards him. Somewhere in the back of her mind it registered that this was partly due to jealousy, but he hadn't been straight with her and she wasn't going to let him make a fool of her again.

She stood up, preparing to leave.

He stood up too. 'I've really blown it, haven't I? I haven't got a chance with you now,' he said, a note of pleading in his voice.

She looked at him, her contempt showing in her eyes.

'I believe we've had this conversation before,' she said, turning to go, 'but I'm not going to fall for it this time.'

He remembered he had said the very same thing about having blown things with her the night he had stayed at her flat.

'Is there *anything* I can say to change your mind?' he asked desperately.

'I trusted you. I believed what you said, even though you'd never given me any reason to trust you,' she said, looking straight at him. 'And one of the great pieces of advice you're so good at handing out, is never to make the same mistake twice.'

He flinched and looked defeated, and she walked away, leaving him standing there watching the door swinging behind her.

It wasn't until she was on her way home that it occurred to her to wonder how he knew the truth about herself and Jack. She concluded that Jack must have told him and shrugged her shoulders. It didn't really matter now anyway.

After Lynsey had walked away from him, James sat for a long time with his pint of beer in front of him, staring into space and trying to accept that there was no way she was ever going to forgive him. It wasn't going to happen and he couldn't really blame her.

He drove home and sat in his car for some time, looking at the outside of the house and thinking about his life and his marriage. It occurred to him that he should be thinking about Lynsey, but it was easier to think about other things; it was less painful. Gina had gone out again. Probably with her friend, Lili. They were always together. She didn't need him any more, for anything. In fact she never had needed him, except as a meal ticket. Having spent years watching Jack and May settling into a happy, married life, he'd been desperate for a steady relationship and Gina had easily trapped him into marrying her (as she had admitted to him, gloatingly, one night when they'd got drunk together, early on in their marriage). He had stayed with her because of the baby, as Gina had known he would. He had been brought up without a father himself and had sworn that he would never abandon any child of his, no matter what the cost to his own life.

He had been very ambitious and had shown signs of being a high flyer after starting work with Jack, and she knew she would have a comfortable life with him. This left her free to pursue her own interests, whatever they were. They had agreed not to interfere with each other's lives and he knew very little about her, really. He did know she was one of the 'ladies who lunch' set and that she entertained frequently. She had never spent a great deal of time with her daughter, either, preferring to lavish her attention on the house, buying antiques and expensive paintings on a regular basis. It had been tough going in the early years, he remembered, trying to cope with all Lisa's needs and paying such a heavy mortgage at the same time, but he had done it and now the house was worth a great deal of money. He estimated it to be worth half a million on the housing market now.

As he gazed morosely at the large, sombre house, he admitted to himself that he had come to hate it; it seemed somehow to symbolise the heavy burden of his marriage. As his thoughts began to take that direction, he thought about Lisa again. She had gone to study at the Glasgow Caledonian University, and she was staying in a flat with her best friend, Jane. He didn't need to keep things together at home for her any more and had known for some time that he was still staying there for no good reason, simply out of habit and because he had nowhere else to go. He had made up his mind. This was something he had looked forward to doing for a long time. He was going to move out – he wanted a divorce and he was going to tell Gina tonight. He might not be able to do anything about Lynsey, but at least he could sort this out, put an end to this farce of a marriage once and for all.

He spent the evening listening out for her arriving home. He was tense, as he had decided to stay sober until he had spoken to her. He wanted her to know he was serious when he told her what was on his mind. He gave her five minutes to settle herself, then walked round to the front of the house and knocked on the door. He was amazed that he felt so apprehensive. It was hardly going to come as a shock to her, was it? They had been building up to this for a long time and there was no love lost between them, as they had never really cared for one another in the first place. But every time he had spoken to Gina in the past she was always so unpleasant and aggressively contemptuous that he hated talking to her about anything. Tonight was no exception, and he stood up straight and braced himself as she opened the door. He looked at her small, squat frame, her short-cropped hair and very dark eyes, and hoped this would be the last time he would have to see her. She stood back to let him in without saying anything and he stood in the middle of the room and coughed uncomfortably.

'Well, get on with it then,' she said impatiently, tipping some Tia Maria into her mouth from a very delicate crystal goblet. She didn't bother to offer him a drink. She sat down on the black leather settee and lit a strong-smelling cigarette – a habit of hers he particularly disliked.

He clenched his teeth and then said baldly: 'I want a divorce.'

She laughed so hard he thought she was going to choke.

'So, the little brunette with the big tits, is it?' she sneered.

She'd noticed the attractive new member of the office the last time she'd gone there to ask for money for a shopping trip.

'What!' he gasped. Her crudity was nothing new to him, but somehow she still managed to disgust him every time they spoke.

'You finally got round to it then, James. I'm quite impressed, didn't think you had it in you.' She stood up and slinked over to him. 'I might even get turned on if you weren't such an ugly little sod.' She grabbed his tie and pulled him towards her roughly, biting down on his lower lip and then pushing him away from her. He covered his lips with his hand as he tasted blood and he glared at her, wondering why he had even done her the courtesy of telling her in person.

'You'll be hearing from my lawyer!' he threw at her as he moved towards the door.

'And you'll be hearing from mine,' Gina replied meaningfully. 'You won't have anything left by the time I'm finished. Get the Merc polished up all nice and shiny. It's mine now!' she shouted at him. Her glass smashed into tiny fragments against the door as soon as it closed behind him.

James went and sat in his car and waited until he felt more composed, then he set off in the direction of Maisie's flat. She'd left her husband a couple of years previously, after the last of her children had left home, and she was in the process of getting a divorce. He clenched his jaw and told himself that it was best to get everything over with in one go. He'd been putting this off for ages because he had become very fond of her over the years and didn't want to hurt her feelings, but it had to be done. To continue his relationship with her now would be unfair to her, given the way he felt about Lynsey. He was well aware, however, that it wouldn't make any difference to Lynsey's opinion of him and that he would probably be completely alone from now on.

Maisie bowed her curly blonde head and became a little tearful when he told her that he felt they shouldn't see each other any more, but he noticed that she didn't seem to be very surprised. Then she blew her nose and sniffed, and told him that someone else had been asking her out for months now and she would say 'yes' the next time he asked.

'You do that, Mais, and I hope it works out for you, I really do,' James said, his voice rather husky with emotion. They kissed affectionately and held each other for a few moments, then he left. There was no point in dragging things out, he felt. He was aware of the irony of the situation, in that he was more upset about saying goodbye to Maisie than he was about ending his marriage.

* * *

Meanwhile, Jack's day was going from bad to worse. He had eaten the chicken and salad, stuffing it into his mouth without really tasting any of it, and he swore under his breath when he realised the whisky bottle was almost empty. He poured out some of Lynsey's wine instead, not caring if mixing his drinks made him sick. Then he noticed a letter with his name on it lying at the top of the mail that had arrived after they'd left for work in the morning. He started to slit open the letter when it occurred to him that there shouldn't be any mail addressed to him at Lynsey's flat. He'd only been there for two weeks and very few people knew he was staying with her. He unfolded the sheets of paper and stared at the formal words in disbelief, which swiftly turned to rage. He clenched his fist and felt his chest tighten as the impact really hit home. *She won't even speak to me and she's doing this! She won't even let me explain, let me sort things out.*

'I don't believe this!' he said out loud, as Lynsey came through the door, closing it noisily behind her and throwing her bag and coat aside.

Although she was hungry and in a very bad mood herself, Lynsey realised almost instantly that there was something very wrong with Jack. She came over to him and he stood up and handed her the papers, still spluttering in anger and disbelief. She read the start of them quickly, registering the fact that he was being sued for divorce, and she tried to put her arms around him, but he was too angry. He pushed her away and started pacing up and down, muttering to himself over and over again that this couldn't be happening.

'Jack—' she began, but he wasn't listening. He just kept pacing back and forth and ignoring her, so she went into the kitchen and made herself a quick sandwich with what was left of the chicken and salad, sighing as she forced herself to eat them. She made two strong coffees and came back into the lounge to give one to Jack, but there was no sign of him. She sighed again as she realised that he had gone to have it out with May, and she knew for certain that he would achieve nothing that night.

15

Comfort

Jack was determined to speak to May and he did. He drove his car right up to the door and banged on one of the bay windows until she had no choice but to open it and speak to him.

'What the hell is this?' he yelled, shaking the letter angrily at her.

'It's over, Jack,' she answered him.

'No, it isn't!' he yelled again. 'Let me come in and we can discuss this sensibly.'

'There's nothing to discuss. It's over,' she told him again.

'May, you're behaving like a teenager.'

'Well, you would know all about that, wouldn't you, Jack, having coped with two of them already,' she added through clenched teeth.

He took a long, slow breath and changed tack. 'Please let me come inside, May; please, I can't bear this.'

'You'll just have to, Jack, because it's not going to change. It's over. I'm done living a lie. I didn't even know I was living a lie, but I do now and it's finished. So go away, because there's nothing you can say that can change things.' She closed the window without waiting to hear his answer.

He stood there for a moment, thinking about what she had said, and as he turned away he saw a large dark shape at the side of the pathway, which he hadn't even noticed before, although he must have driven straight past it. As he stood looking at it in a daze, he realised that it was a heap of bags, some of them luggage and others simply heavy-duty bin bags. He walked over to them, knowing before he opened them that his belongings were inside. Automatically, he bent down and started shifting them into the boot of his car, his rage roiling in his chest all the while. She would regret this, he was sure. Once she'd had time to cool down and realise what she'd done, she'd regret it. There was no way this was a permanent arrangement. He would take his things for the moment, because he needed them, and because May would leave them outside in all weathers if he didn't shift them, but he realised now that things weren't going to sort themselves out and he needed help as soon as possible.

As he drove home, he made up his mind to do something about the situation the next day, as soon as he got up, because for the first time in his life, he didn't know how to deal with what was happening; he couldn't control things the way he usually did. It was a difficult thing for him to admit, but he was no fool and he realised that he was too emotionally involved to tackle the situation rationally. When he arrived at the flat he told Lynsey he was moving out. He said he couldn't impose on her any longer because May was still being difficult and he didn't know how long it would be before she would 'see sense', as he put it.

'You're not going anywhere tonight, Dad,' she protested, looking at him in dismay, 'It's Christmas Eve!'

She told him to bring his bags indoors and they would sort something out in the morning. He looked exhausted and she helped him to bring his things into the narrow hallway.

'That's a lot of stuff, Jack,' she commented.

He grunted. 'It's only temporary,' he assured her, 'She'll come round eventually.' He went into the other room and closed the door without even saying goodnight and she got ready for bed slowly and sadly, very much afraid that 'eventually' might be longer than Jack realised.

The two of them spent a very quiet, subdued Christmas Day together and Lynsey carefully hid Julia's present in the back of a cupboard in her bedroom so that Jack wouldn't see it. She was glad her mother had had enough sense to stay away from them, for the time being at any rate.

* * *

The next few weeks were rather difficult. Jack had made an announcement in the office to let everyone know that John and Lynsey were his son and daughter, and although it didn't seem to change anyone's attitude towards John, because he had been working there for a while, it was different for Lynsey. She was aware that no one wanted to confide in her so much any more, and she couldn't really blame them. They were obviously worried that she would carry tales back to her father. Jack was no further forward with May, even after seeing a solicitor and having a long heart-to-heart with Lynsey to ask her advice on what to do for the best. He asked her to help him and she told him she had been trying to get in touch with May, but couldn't even get to speak to her.

'But you're usually so good at this kind of thing, Lynsey,' he complained, 'pouring oil on troubled waters.'

'I'm too close to this, Dad, too involved. Let's face it, your daughter is the last person May wants to talk to right now.'

The anger seemed to seep out of him as she told him this, and tears came into his eyes. 'It will be all right in the end, though, won't it, love?' he asked pathetically.

'I don't know, Dad,' she answered. She wasn't being totally honest with him. Deep down inside she was beginning to feel certain it wouldn't be all right at all, not in the foreseeable future, anyway.

* * *

During the following week in the office, Lynsey's spirits were very low and Nick kept coming over and trying to cheer her up. One afternoon when there weren't many people around, he asked her out again and this time she accepted. The situation with Jack and the deadlock with James had combined to make her feel rather depressed and unsure of herself. She needed an escape and a bit of time to just relax, unwind and enjoy herself. It wouldn't do any harm, she was sure, so long as she made it clear to him that it was on a 'no strings' basis.

He agreed eagerly and said he understood and that a casual basis was fine with him, too. She suspected that wasn't entirely true, but she did cheer up a little as she thought of having some time away from the stresses and tensions surrounding her life. She was vaguely aware of James watching them together, but she wasn't going to sit at home feeling miserable just because he was jealous! As far as she was concerned, she and James could continue to speak to each other as little as possible, discussing business formally and coldly, and avoiding each other most of the time. He'd made his bed and he could lie in it – alone!

Lynsey and Nick went out that evening to a Chinese restaurant in Almada Street and had a very enjoyable evening together. Just before they left, Lynsey went to the Ladies and when she came back out of the cubicle there were two women standing in front of the sinks, kissing and fondling each other. When they noticed Lynsey, one of them – a small, square-boned woman with dark, beady eyes – smiled and winked at her, and Lynsey washed her hands as quickly as possible and left, feeling slightly embarrassed. A couple of women kissing each other she wouldn't have minded, but they were all over each other and it had made her feel quite uncomfortable.

Aside from this little incident, she was surprised at how much she had enjoyed the date, and when Nick invited her to his place afterwards, she was quite happy to go. He had a really nice flat and his flatmate was staying overnight with his girlfriend, so they had the place to themselves. They had a few drinks and listened to music. Their tastes were fairly similar and after a while

Nick put on a disc of slow, romantic ballads. He took her hand and drew her up onto the floor to dance and they started to kiss. Lynsey was attracted to him and wondered if she should just throw caution to the wind and stop agonising about everything. She had almost decided to do that when her mind went back to the night James had stayed with her and she just froze.

'I'm sorry, Nick, I can't,' she said, trying to explain to him that it wasn't going to work. She thought he would be annoyed, but he just smiled and shrugged.

'Hey, I understand, Lynsey. But you can't blame a guy for trying, can you?' he asked with a cheeky grin.

'The thing is, Nick, I do like being with you,' she said apologetically, 'but I don't know if there can be anything else between us. I'm sort of hung up on someone else.'

'I don't mind if you want to just be friends, Lynsey. Honestly, it's fine by me,' he said easily.

He was being very understanding, but Lynsey wasn't sure she really believed him.

'I don't want to lead you on, Nick. I might feel differently later, but I don't know if I will. Maybe it's best if we don't see each other.'

He shrugged his shoulders. 'Is that what you want?' he asked quietly.

'No, it isn't, Nick, but it wouldn't be fair to you ...'

'Well, how about if we hang out together for a while and just see how it goes?' he asked carefully. *She's worth waiting for*, he thought, *and if it doesn't work out, there's no harm done.*

'Are you sure?' she asked uncertainly.

'Sure I'm sure,' he said, tweaking her nose affectionately.

'OK then,' she agreed, 'we'll do that.' She looked at him and realised that he wasn't emotionally involved with her, after all, and that she really needed some TLC. If he had been difficult about things or had become moody and cold after she'd said she wanted to keep things platonic between them, she would have put on her coat and left, there and then. As it was, she felt convinced now that he wasn't falling for her and she was sure neither of them would get hurt when things ended between them. She looked at him speculatively.

'Here's to us!' he said, picking up his glass and toasting her.

'To us!' Lynsey answered, raising her own glass and smiling for the first time in weeks.

'Nick – let's go to bed,' she said, making him stare at her with a puzzled frown.

'But I thought you didn't want to …'

'I changed my mind,' she said simply.

'Well, that's fine by me' he said, grinning broadly.

To hell with Jim Bolton, she thought, *he's not the only one who needs some comfort.*

Nick took her hand and they went through to his bedroom. She discovered he was a very considerate lover and she was glad she'd changed her mind. She hadn't been prepared for this to happen tonight, however, and a niggly little worry regarding contraception went through her mind. She promised herself she would sort it out later and she just tuned everything else out and made the most of the night.

16

Divorce

January dragged by slowly, as it invariably does. In the office, the workload had quietened down and the staff were fairly quiet, too, except for Lynsey and Nick, who were now dating steadily.

Jack was actually becoming quite morose, and Lynsey was becoming more and more concerned about him. Things had gone from bad to worse with May and he had threatened to force her to let him back into the house, pointing out that he was legally entitled to live there. Besides which, he maintained, he had done nothing to harm her and he never would. When she had finally allowed him to come inside the house to talk to her, he had put these things to her and she had informed him coldly that if he came back to live in the house she would simply leave and disappear and he would never see her again. He had left then, feeling despair settle over him like a heavy blanket. What was he going to do? There was no way out. There was too much of a barrier between them. She was going to divorce him and he couldn't think of any way of stopping her. He had sent her flowers, hundreds of them, with cards telling her how much he loved her, but there were no flowers to be seen when he was inside the house and she had looked at him as if he were a salesman trying to sell her expensive goods that she didn't want.

The winter weeks passed with no respite in the weather or in Jack's marital situation. By the middle of March he was taking days off work for no real reason. He was still living in Lynsey's flat with her. He had intended finding somewhere else to stay, at first, but she had urged him to stay with her as long as he needed to, and he had no enthusiasm for finding a place of his own, without May. So he stayed on, and his despair was no longer just a blanket around him; it had somehow seeped into his very bones, sapping all strength from his heart and mind. His brain didn't seem to function properly any more. He couldn't concentrate on work and couldn't get interested in or excited about anything.

One Friday morning he awoke after a restless night and simply pulled the duvet over his head again. *Why bother getting up?* he thought. It all seemed so pointless now. He heard Lynsey calling to him through the door of his room that it was time for work. He stayed where he was and closed his eyes again. He didn't need to eat or drink as he wasn't hungry or thirsty, and there was nothing he wanted to do. When Lynsey eventually opened the door, trying to coax him out of bed, he pretended to be asleep until she left him alone. He heard her leaving the flat. Sleep would claim him again soon, he was so tired these days. If it didn't, he'd take more of those pills the doctor had given him. Sleep was good – it blotted out the emptiness in his heart.

* * *

When Lynsey arrived at the office she walked straight past Marcia's desk without saying good morning to her, or even noticing her, and was so worried about Jack that even when she started her work she couldn't concentrate on anything. She kept snapping at people over nothing, especially James. He was being quite civil to her these days, as she had always wanted him to be, but ironically, this only served to irritate her even more. Since she had started work there, everyone had come to expect her to be cheery and helpful, but now they all sat quietly, trying not to upset her. Several of her colleagues had remarked to James that something was wrong with her, and he said he would look into it.

He sent her an email asking her to come into his office for 'a word'. She stood up and marched belligerently into his room and looked at him without saying anything. He knew he was going to have to tread very carefully. As she stood there looking at him, he was aware of there being something different about her appearance, but couldn't quite put his finger on what it was.

'Sit down, Lynsey, please,' he said. She sat, reluctantly.

'I see Jack isn't at work again today,' he remarked. 'Is he OK?'

'Oh, he's on top of the world, what do you think?' she snapped back.

She was skirting the edges of acceptable treatment of one's boss, but he wasn't about to make an issue of it. After a moment's thoughtful silence, he tried again.

'Lynsey, this can't go on, you know that. Has Jack given up on May or what? I thought they'd be back together again by now. What's the problem?'

'Oh, I don't really know,' she said sarcastically. 'She seems to be upset about him having a whole other life and two kids she didn't know anything about. Silly really, isn't it?'

'Lynsey, I'm trying to be reasonable, but I can't let things go on like this. I'm covering for Jack all the time, but clients are starting to notice, and I'm trying to be civil to you and all I get is this attitude from you all the time.'

'Now you know how it feels,' she threw back, giving him a hard stare.

'Is that what you're doing, getting revenge? Making me pay?'

'Don't give me that,' she said. 'The only reason you're being "civil" to me is because now you know I'm the boss's daughter!'

His back straightened indignantly.

'You know that's not .... anyway, he's not *my* boss, we're partners – it isn't that ...' His voice tailed off. It was hopeless. He knew how things must look to her. He realised miserably that they had come full circle. Their attitudes towards each other were the reverse of what they had been before, and she wasn't handling it any better than he had! She was thinking the worst of him the way he had done with her, proving that she wasn't 'Little Miss Perfect' after all. But it was cold comfort.

She stood up to leave and he let her go without saying any more. There was no point. He was *persona non grata* to her now and always would be, no matter what he said to her. He had blown the only chance he'd ever had of finding happiness. He'd done it arrogantly and callously and there was no going back. He watched her sit down heavily at her desk and start immediately thumping the keyboard. She was a different person from the happy, easy-going woman she had been just a few months ago. He wished with all his heart she could be like that again. He knew she was worried about Jack, as he was, but even if that situation resolved itself, he didn't hold out much hope that she would ever view him any differently from the way she did now. He turned and walked over to look out of the window, as he tended to do when something was troubling him. It usually soothed him and helped him to get a perspective on things, but nothing soothed him these days.

His heart was full of love for a woman who despised him. He finally admitted to himself that he'd always had feelings for her, right from the start, and that that was why he'd behaved like an idiot. He now lived in constant fear of the very thing he had wanted so much when she first came to work there – that she would decide to leave and he'd hardly ever see her again. There would be no chance to try to make things better between them; he would lose her for good. To make matters worse, she and Nick were a solid couple now. There was nothing he could do. Whichever angle he looked at it from, it was stalemate.

17

Jack's Breakdown

While James was gazing out of his office window, Julia was putting the finishing touches to her make-up. Then she dabbed herself with Poison and lit a cigarette. She was full of nervous excitement, as if she were about to give a performance on stage. It was time to make a move. She had given him long enough to get over the break-up and she was beginning to run out of money. Tony had been good to her while they were together, but he had left her with very little except for the house. If things got any worse, she'd have to think about finding a job! It was time to get things moving. It had taken her years to talk Tony into tying the knot, so she was prepared to put in some time and effort for a bigger prize.

She knew she looked her best. She'd just had her hair done and her sense of anticipation lent a soft flush to her cheeks that enhanced her still-smooth complexion. She tweaked her top to make sure she was showing just the right amount of cleavage. She had let Jack slip through her fingers once before, and hadn't pursued him further as she had met Tony soon afterwards. But it had always been Jack for her, she told herself, and now that he was no longer with May, or any woman as far as she could gather, he was a sitting duck, so to speak. Men were so predictable for her normally, but Jack had rejected her before, so she was a little unsure of herself, and this added to her tension.

She hadn't heard from Lynsey since it had all 'hit the fan', but she had managed to glean a few details from John when she'd called him earlier in the week, so she knew Jack would be at the flat. It was Friday, so Lynsey would be working. *Perfect*, she thought. She knew what she wanted and she was sure she was about to get it.

It was a lovely, sunny day and she set off in high spirits and arrived in Uddingston in record time. She parked her car round the corner from the flat. With a bit of luck she wouldn't need it until the next day! She pictured herself heading off into the sunset with Jack and wondered if Lynsey would be surprised. She knocked at the door of the flat, but there was no answer, so she kept on knocking until all the neighbours came to their doors, but still Jack didn't answer. However, the commotion had roused him and he dragged himself out of bed to go to the toilet. He heard all the voices outside and put on his robe before pulling the door open. He stood there in astonishment as the neighbours disappeared back into their flats and Julia strode into the hallway.

'Hi there!' she said, as if they'd just met in a bar. 'Well, aren't you going to offer me a drink?' she asked hopefully. He was speechless, but not for long.

'What the hell do *you* want?' he snarled.

Julia was taken aback by his dishevelled appearance, and a combination of weight loss and stress had hollowed out his face, but she wasn't going to let anything stop her now.

'A drink and some company would be nice,' she answered sweetly, as if his question had been serious. 'Why don't you get changed and then we can go somewhere?' she suggested.

He stared at her as if she was a madwoman. He was trying to decide if it was Julia who was mad or himself, for standing there listening to her. He moved right in front of her and pushed his face into hers. Everything that had happened with May was Julia's fault, as far as he was concerned, and a tornado of emotion began to twist inside him.

'Julia, if you don't leave here right now, I might have to kill you,' he said grittily. 'In fact,' he added through clenched teeth, 'I might just do that anyway.'

She stepped back a little and opened her mouth to speak, but thought better of it. Obviously she had misjudged the situation, but that didn't give him the right to talk to her like that. She tried to placate him.

'There's no need to—' she began, but he grabbed her arm and shoved her roughly out of the door.

'All of this is down to you, you *bitch!*' he shouted at her back. 'If you come anywhere near me or May again it'll be the last thing you ever do!' he roared, slamming the door so hard the whole building shook.

Julia had been shoved out of the door so fast she only just managed to stop herself from falling down the stairs, and she had to stand on the top step for a moment to get her breath back. Then she straightened herself up in case anyone was watching her, ran down the steps and round the corner, out of sight, to fling herself moodily back into her car. She wouldn't be back here again, that was for sure. She sat and smoked another cigarette to steady her nerves and considered her options. *He's not the only fish in the sea and I've always looked out for myself. Who does he think he is anyway, talking to me like that!* She sighed, feeling really annoyed. *I'll just have to try and get Tony back instead, she decided. What a damn nuisance!*

* * *

Inside the flat, Jack was struggling to cope with his fury. His life with May was over, and all because of *her. She rips my life apart and then she swans in here like nothing's happened!* The more he tried to contain his rage the more it spiralled out of control. He felt as if something had burst inside him. He couldn't hold everything in any longer and he stormed into the lounge, waving his arms and roaring in fury. Lynsey had recently put up an old photo of Jack, John and herself enjoying a day out, and the edge of his sleeve caught it and hurled it to the floor. He stood and looked down at the broken glass, then picked up the frame. He drew the picture out, let go of the frame, and tore the photo slowly in half, straight down the middle. For some reason, this seemed to ease his feelings a little. He dropped the photo and looked around, seeing some newspapers and magazines on the coffee table. He lifted one of the papers and began tearing it up. He tore it into shreds. The smaller the pieces, the better he felt.

Somewhere in the back of his mind he was aware that this was not normal behaviour and that Lynsey would be upset, but he couldn't seem to stop himself now. It was like a compulsion; once he'd started he had to keep going, deriving some strange sort of satisfaction from it. He couldn't stop and he didn't even want to. Soon, the mound of tiny pieces of paper began to cover his feet and ankles. When he couldn't find any more he sat down on the settee and grabbed as much of the shredded paper as he could into his hands, bunching it all into tight balls inside his fists. He took slow deep breaths through his nose and stared straight ahead of him, all the while clutching the paper tighter and tighter, his teeth clenched and his lips pressed tightly together.

Almost two hours later, Lynsey came home from work and thought that Jack must be in bed when she saw there were no lights on. She was aware of the silence as she walked along the hall and went into the lounge. She found him sitting there, heaps of torn paper everywhere. He didn't even seem to realise that she was there, talking to him.

'Oh my God, Dad, what are you doing?' she whispered, knowing that he wouldn't answer her. She knew now that he really was heading for a breakdown and she gently took hold of his arm and led him into his bedroom. She helped him to lie on the bed and then covered him with the duvet. He closed his eyes and was soon breathing evenly, exhaustion taking its toll. She left his room and went back to the lounge, intending to clear up the mess, but after a few minutes she sat down and began to cry, her own misery and Jack's despair merging inside her all at once. She gave in to the onslaught and wept softly, with a feeling of hopelessness, until she eventually fell asleep.

* * *

She was awakened later in the evening by noises coming from Jack's room. Then there was a loud bump and she sat up very straight and listened. She could hear him moving about and she stood up, some of the paper still clinging to her clothes and shoes, and went to see what was going on. She gingerly opened the door of his room and was shocked by what she saw. He was walking slowly round the room taking the posters off the walls and tearing them up. She spoke to him, begging him to stop, but it was as if he couldn't hear her. She went through to the lounge again, and the shards of broken glass on the carpet made her aware that this situation could easily get out of hand. She was afraid that he was going to hurt himself, or her, before the night was over.

She took a tissue and blew her nose, then shakily lifted the phone. She needed help, but she didn't know whom she should call. John and Marcia had gone to stay with her parents for the weekend and there was no way she was calling Julia. Not Nick either; she didn't want him to see her father like this, and she knew Jack wouldn't want that either. She hesitated long enough to hear something crashing to the floor in Jack's room and called the Enquiries number to get James's home number. She asked them to put her straight through, and as she listened to it ringing out, she tried to calm herself enough to be able to explain things to him. *Please be in, please be in*, she prayed as she waited for him to pick up.

* * *

James lay on top of his bed, fully clothed, listening to the telephone ringing and wondering who it could possibly be, at this hour on a Friday night. He'd had enough whisky to not really care, but the extension was right beside the bed and it kept on ringing. Eventually, he reached over and answered it. The last voice in the world he expected to hear answered him and he sat bolt upright and listened intently. She wasn't hysterical but was obviously very distressed, babbling something about Jack. There was no way he could drive tonight, so he said, slowly and carefully, 'OK, Lynsey. I'm leaving right now. I'll be there as soon as I can.'

He hung up and dialled the local taxi number. While he waited for the cab, he splashed his face, combed his hair and threw on his jacket, wondering what was wrong and trying not to panic at the thought of Lynsey being in any danger. He'd heard some noises in the background, but Jack surely wouldn't hurt her, would he? There was no time for a black coffee, but on the way to the flat he reflected that he had never sobered up so quickly in his life. Fear blots out everything else, and the instinct to protect yourself and those closest to your heart is very strong.

When he arrived at the flat, he ran up the stairs two at a time and turned the door handle without knocking. The door opened and Lynsey stopped pacing up and down and came towards him.

'I'm sorry for phoning you,' she said, 'I didn't know what else to do. I don't know how to stop him – he won't listen to me.'

'Is he in there?' he asked, pointing to the door of Jack's room, where Jack was moving about and seemed to be talking to someone. She nodded. The door was ajar and he pushed it open. Jack was wandering around muttering to himself. The floor was strewn with paper and clothes that had been pulled out of the open drawers. James spoke to him, but when he got no reply he went over and put his hand on Jack's shoulder. Jack stopped, looked at James as though he were a stranger and carried on muttering to himself. James took his mobile out of his pocket and asked Lynsey for the name of Jack's GP.

'It's Dr Smart, but do you think we should get the doctor involved?' she asked uncertainly. 'It'll be on his record then.'

'I think we have to, Lynsey. I can't see this sorting itself out.'

She nodded worriedly. He rang the doctor's number and asked for an emergency visit. Jack was obviously having some sort of breakdown. He stayed with him until the doctor arrived, to make sure he didn't do himself or Lynsey any harm. The doctor gave Jack an injection to sedate him and they put him to bed together.

'He'll sleep now,' he told them, 'but don't leave him on his own. I'll come back first thing to see how he's doing.' Lynsey nodded and thanked him.

He left and James turned to speak to her. She'd gone back into the lounge and was sitting on the settee looking down at something in her hands. He walked over to her and sat down beside her.

'Lynsey?' he asked tentatively. She was holding a photograph of Jack, John and a girl who was obviously Lynsey, although her hair looked much lighter than it was now. The colour was exactly like John's and it was wavy like John's, too. He realised that this was the change he had noticed in her appearance recently, although her hair was still quite a bit darker than it was in the photograph.

'He tore it up,' she whispered, the tears running down her cheeks. 'How could he do that?'

It was obviously important to her and he said gently, 'He's not himself, Lynsey. He probably didn't mean to tear it.'

She carried on crying. He hesitated, then put his arm around her shoulders. 'It can be fixed, you know. You can get them fixed as good as new these days,' he said consolingly. She put her head on his shoulder and closed her eyes.

'Jack's asleep now, so you should try and get some sleep, too,' he suggested. She nodded. He stood up to go.

'Jim,' she called out after him. He turned round. 'Thank you,' she said. 'I don't know what I'd have done if you hadn't come over.'

'That's OK,' he assured her. 'Don't worry, you did the right thing. I'll come back in the morning and see how he is. I'll see myself out.'

She looked despairingly at the mess and he watched her trudge wearily into her room, obviously worn out. He looked around the room at all the paper and broken glass. Then he took his jacket off again, went to look for bin bags and a brush and shovel and started to clear up, as quietly as he could. Twenty minutes later he left, feeling really tired himself, but glad she wouldn't have to wake up to a disaster area in the morning. There would be enough for her to deal with without that.

18

Building Bridges

Not surprisingly, Lynsey slept late the following morning and left her room very tentatively, putting on her slippers in case she stood on any glass. There was no sound coming from Jack's room, so she had a quick bowl of cereal in the kitchen and gulped down half a cup of coffee before going into the lounge to begin clearing up. When she opened the door she stood there in amazement, wondering if she had dreamt it all. She hurried along to Jack's room and tears came into her eyes as she looked at the mess and wondered if he would be back to normal when he woke up. He was still sleeping heavily and she breathed a sigh of relief. She closed the door again and then remembered that the bin in the kitchen had looked very full. *Jim*, she thought. *He must have cleared up last night before he left.*

She went into the bathroom and took a refreshing shower, then dressed quickly in jeans and a black jersey. She had remembered about the photograph and was just about to start rummaging through the bucket to find it when someone knocked at the door and she knew it was James. She stood back to let him in and he asked about Jack.

'He's still asleep,' she told him anxiously. 'I hope the doctor hasn't overdone the sedative,' she added, frowning a little.

'It's probably exhaustion as well,' he said.

She nodded. 'Yes, he hasn't been sleeping properly since he and May…' she tailed off. They looked at each other awkwardly. She cleared her throat and asked if he would like to take off his jacket and have a coffee.

'Thanks' he said. He'd just had one before he left home, but it would give them something to do.

'Thanks for clearing up last night, Jim,' she said as she went to put the kettle on. 'I wondered if I'd imagined it all when I saw the lounge earlier.'

He took off his jacket. They smiled at each other sheepishly because he was wearing jeans and a black jersey, too! As she took his jacket to hang it up, James remembered the last time she had done that, when he'd stayed all night. He hadn't thought then that he would ever be welcome in this flat again, nor ever want to come into it again, for that matter. He felt a little awkward, so he went through to the lounge and sat down. She brought the coffees through, but she didn't sit next to him this time, she sat down in the chair opposite him.

He took a couple of sips of his coffee, then to break the silence he drew the torn photograph out of his back trouser pocket.

'Oh, by the way, just in case you go searching for this, I've got it here,' he told her. She went to take it from him, but he held onto it and put it back in his pocket. 'I'll get it fixed for you,' he said.

'It's OK, I can do that myself,' she told him.

'It's no bother,' he insisted. 'You've enough on your plate, I think.' He didn't think things would ever come right between them, after all that had happened, but it made him feel better just to help her when she needed it and to be able to speak with her almost normally. There was still a long way to go, but at least the ice was broken now.

He looked at the photograph again. 'You should lighten your hair again,' he said, 'it suits you.'

She didn't respond to that. She wasn't about to have him telling her what to do or not do with her appearance.

'I'd better see how Jack is now,' she said stiffly, draining her cup and taking it with her into the kitchen. James looked more closely at the picture in his hand and slowly it dawned on him that the colour of her hair was natural – it was the dark colour that was false! She'd darkened it so that no one would connect her with John or Jack. As he sat there thinking that dying her hair was a bit over the top, he was struck by the extent of the resemblance between her and her brother. *They're twins*, he realised suddenly. It seemed plausible to him now that someone might well have spotted the resemblance between them if she had left her appearance as it was.

On her way back from the kitchen, Lynsey went into Jack's room. He was awake, but he just lay there, staring at the ceiling. She went over and sat on the edge of his bed.

'Dad,' she asked softly, 'are you feeling a bit better this morning?'

He just kept staring at the ceiling and didn't even turn round to look at her. She wasn't sure if he'd heard her.

'Dad!' she said again, a little louder. There was no response. She put a hand on his shoulder, but he didn't seem to be aware of it. She was beginning to get angry with him and she sighed in exasperation and left the room, leaving the door a little ajar. Jim joined her in the hallway.

'Is he still out cold?' he asked quietly, seeing her face.

'No, he's awake, but he won't speak to me,' she said, her voice trembling a little.

'What about if I have a try?' he asked her.

'Well, it can't do any harm,' she said, shrugging her shoulders. 'I'm obviously not getting through to him.'

James came back out of the bedroom a few minutes later and as he passed the front door, there was a loud knocking. It was Dr Smart. They both told him that Jack wasn't responding to them and he went in to see for himself. When he came back out he said that Jack was suffering from severe depression and nervous exhaustion and that it would be best not to leave him on his own for any length of time.

'But he will get better, won't he?' Lynsey asked him anxiously.

'In time,' the doctor told her. 'He has no history of depression or nervous illness, so I'm assuming this was brought on by something specific.'

'Yes,' Lynsey told him, 'he and May have separated.'

'Ah,' he answered. 'well, that will take a bit of getting used to, but once things pick up he should rally again and get back to his old self. It'll need time and patience, though.'

'How long is he going to be like this, do you think?' she asked.

'Very difficult to say,' he told her. He looked at his watch and said he had to go. Lynsey nodded and showed him out. James lifted his jacket off the hook and headed for the door.

'I'd best be going as well,' he said. 'I'll come back later today, if that's all right, to see how he's doing.'

'Right, fine. See you later then,' she answered. She felt awkward with him there, but at the same time, she didn't want him to leave.

He headed off to see about getting a replacement photograph for her. He settled himself in his car, took the old photograph out of his pocket and looked at it again. He sighed. He couldn't have misjudged the situation more when he'd jumped to conclusions about Lynsey and Jack, and he would have to live with the results of his behaviour for a long time.

Although his heart was heavy with regret, he was determined to make things up to her and to give her as much support as he could with her father. Jack Forrest having a breakdown! He still couldn't believe it. James was facing difficult times himself, with Gina making the most of the divorce by trying to screw every last penny out of him. Also, he urgently needed to get out of that house and find a new place to live before too much longer. As if all that wasn't enough, he was having to shoulder Jack's workload, too. It occurred to him that he would have to be careful he didn't start heading towards meltdown himself!

19

An Idea

A little later, James drove home with the new photograph in his jacket pocket. It had turned out much better than he'd hoped and he'd had an extra two copies made. He would give a spare one to Lynsey and keep one for himself, he decided. He wasn't sure if that was a bit sad, but he didn't care. She would never know he had it, would she? He gazed at it, thinking how lovely she looked, and wondered how she could ever have been interested in him. Obviously she could have anyone she wanted.

When he arrived home he found Lisa waiting for him on the doorstep.

'Lisa, you should have called!' he said delightedly, giving her a big hug.

'How long have you been waiting?'

'Not long, Dad. I wanted to surprise you.'

'Well, you managed it,' he answered, smiling. 'How long are you staying?'

'Um, I thought I'd stay overnight if that's OK?'

'Of course it's OK.' He grinned at her. 'Why wouldn't it be?'

'Well, you might have had company planned,' she said, looking enquiringly at him.

'Not at all. And even if I did, I'd soon cancel it to have you here instead,' he assured her.

She noticed the tip of the photograph sleeve sticking out of his pocket.

'What's the photos, Dad?' she asked.

'Oh, nothing interesting,' he answered, waving his hand dismissively.

She raised her eyebrows but didn't pursue it. While he prepared some lunch they chatted light-heartedly about her life at Uni and her new friends. She mentioned one name quite a few times and he asked her if she had anything to tell him. She blushed and looked away, but she was smiling.

'Not yet,' she said happily. 'What about you, Dad?' she asked, trying to change the subject. Have *you* anything to tell *me*?'

He hesitated. She had a right to know, but he wasn't sure how she would react and he didn't want to upset her.

'Lisa, I've spoken to your mother. Now that you've left home ... I – the thing is, we're getting divorced,' he said, as gently as he could.

She stopped eating for a moment and then took a long drink from her glass of water.

'I thought that might happen once I left.' She began eating again and he thought it best to try to explain things a little, but she interrupted him.

'Dad, you don't have to explain – I understand. You only stayed for my sake, I've known that for a long time.' She paused. 'Will you stay here or are you going to move away?'

'I think I'll probably leave, but I don't have any idea where to go. I'll have to start looking for something soon, though. This place is getting me down.

'I don't know how you've stuck it for so long, I really don't,' she said.

'Have you seen your mother yet?' he asked.

'No, not yet. I'll pop round tomorrow.'

'That's fine, I'll be going out for a while tomorrow, and I'd feel bad if you were on your own,' he told her.

'Oh, where are you off to then – Maisie's?'

'No, actually.' He stopped speaking and she noticed he looked a little flushed. 'I'm going round to Lynsey's flat to see Jack. He's not keeping very well just now.'

'Jack's at Lynsey's flat? She was amazed. 'Why? And what's wrong with him?' she asked.

'It's a bit of a long story, Lisa. We called the doctor out for him last night and I'm quite worried about him.'

'We?' she asked, with a puzzled frown.

'Me and Lynsey. She rang and asked me to come over. She was in a bit of a state and didn't know what else to do. Jack was in a world of his own – he was wrecking the place. You know I told you about him and May on the phone? Well, he's just not coping with it. We think he's having some sort of breakdown actually, but maybe he'll settle down again soon. I hope so.'

'Oh, Dad, the poor man.' She had noticed how he'd said 'we' again about himself and Lynsey.

'A break-up's the worst thing that could have happened, for him, but for you and mum it's been a long time coming and it'll make you feel so much better.'

He smiled a little. When had his daughter become so grown-up? She sounded more like twenty-eight than eighteen.

'I don't know about that. I think Gina will do her best to bankrupt me!' he said, laughing a little shakily. She smiled back at him, trying to reassure him, but she knew this would mean big changes in his life and that he must feel very unsure of the future.

Next day, shortly before lunchtime, Lisa went round to the front of the house to visit her mother and James left to go and see Lynsey and Jack. When he arrived at the flat, he almost expected Jack to be striding around the flat demanding to know what all the fuss was about, but he wasn't.

Lynsey opened the door to James and as soon as he saw her face he knew Jack was no better. He went into the bedroom to see him and tried to get a response from him, but he lay on his front, keeping very still and not speaking, and it was impossible to tell if he was awake or not. James left him in peace and went to find

Lynsey. She was in the kitchen taking juice out of the fridge and thinking how much she would prefer a large glass of wine. She looked pale and tired and James stood behind her and asked if she was all right.

'Not really,' she answered him. 'I'd love some wine, but I don't have any left. Mother was right, I should keep more in the house so I don't run out.'

Thinking of Julia made her angry all over again and she banged her glass down on the table.

'This is all her fault. How could she do this to him? I'll never forgive her.' She stopped speaking and blinked rapidly so that she wouldn't start crying again. She was getting as bad as Jack! She didn't want James to think *she* was cracking up, too.

'Have you eaten anything?' he asked her.

'Yes,' she said, 'there was a pizza in the freezer. I tried to get Jack to eat something, even just some soup, but he wouldn't even answer me.'

'Dr Smart will be here to see him again in the morning. He won't come to any harm before then. Lynsey, would you like me to bring in some wine for you? I think you need to wind down.'

'What if Jack gets up?' she asked.

'I'm here to see to him if he does,' he assured her. 'I'm driving, so one whisky from Jack's bottle will do me fine.'

'Well, if you're sure,' she said.

He went to the nearby off-licence and was back within ten minutes. She had poured him a glass of whisky with a little water and he handed her the bottle of wine and a new bottle of whisky for Jack.

'You didn't need to do that,' she told him.

'I had a couple from his bottle yesterday and now I'm using up the last of it, so it's the least I can do,' he told her.

She switched on the television and they sat together as the afternoon drew on into evening. They watched a couple of game shows and then a movie came on that they had both seen before.

'I don't mind if you switch channels,' she said to him. 'I'm not really much bothered, to tell you the truth.'

He lifted the remote control and began to check the listings. He was glad Jack was quiet, as he was enjoying the peace. He realised that, ironically, if it hadn't been for Jack's troubles, which had come between James and Lynsey in the first place, he wouldn't be sitting here spending the evening with her now.

'Lynsey—' he began, feeling the need to clear the air a little.

She held up her hand to stop him.

'James, it's all in the past. It was a misunderstanding, that's all.'

He sighed with relief and smiled a little. Maybe things weren't hopeless after all. However, his thoughts came to an abrupt halt as the tranquillity was shattered by someone ringing the doorbell. Lynsey went to answer it.

A moment later the visitor came into the lounge. It was John, obviously here to tell Lynsey all about the visit with his future in-laws. He saw James and stopped speaking in mid-sentence.

'What the hell,' he muttered, then he turned and looked at Lynsey as if to say, *Are you out of your mind?*

'John, ' Lynsey said, 'we've had a problem with Jack. He's not well at all.'

The 'we' wasn't lost on him. He turned to James and told him to get out.

'There's no need for that!' Lynsey said. 'James's been helping me.'

'I bet he has,' he growled. 'You can leave now,' he said loudly to James. 'If Lynsey or Jack need anything, I'm here.'

Lynsey looked at James unhappily, and he left without making a fuss and went straight home.

He went round to the back door, hoping that Lisa was still with her mother. He felt he needed some time to collect his thoughts before he spoke to his daughter. He poured enough whisky to keep him going for a while and then sat down in his favourite chair. His thoughts weren't pleasant.

He was aware that the tension between himself and Lynsey had lessened considerably since Jack's brainstorm, but John's attitude tonight had given him a reality check. John wasn't easily going to forget James's earlier treatment of Lynsey, and now that

James understood John's protectiveness towards her, things looked even bleaker than before. *The whole thing's just a mess*, he thought, closing his eyes and putting his hand over his face.

A sudden voice made him jump. Lisa had come back in.

'Dad, what is it? What's wrong? Is it Jack?'

'No, no, Jack's just the same,' he said miserably. 'It's … complicated,' he said, not knowing where to start, and not sure if he should be burdening her with his problems. She sat down beside him and gave him an 'old-fashioned' look and he knew he was going to tell her everything. It might not do any good, but at least he would get it off his chest.

Some time later, he put his head back and closed his eyes again, waiting for her to tell him unconvincingly that everything would be fine, that love would conquer all, etc etc.

'You know what you need to do, Dad, you need to go see May,' she said with assurance.

He opened his eyes and looked at her, blinking. 'May?'

She nodded.

'What for?' he said stupidly.

She didn't answer him, just raised her eyebrows and shook her head. He thought about it. In his preoccupation with Lynsey, he had forgotten who was really the injured party in all of this – the woman who was sitting alone right now – miserable, betrayed, separated from her husband, and probably friendless into the bargain, because of all the years she had devoted to her marriage. There was no secret lover waiting to step into Jack's shoes, and her own family had broken contact with her when she'd defied them and married Jack, because he was so much older than herself and a 'playboy' into the bargain. May had no one, and she found herself in this situation through no fault of her own. *And I'm as bad as the rest*, he thought. He had forgotten about her, too, wrapped up in his own troubles. He felt a stab of guilt. He was probably her only friend, her boyfriend of many years ago, and he hadn't even contacted her to tell her how sorry he was about her and Jack.

May needed some support and maybe he could let her know how much Jack was suffering, too. *It might mean a breakthrough for them if I handle it carefully*, he thought hopefully. If there was one thing knowing Lynsey had taught him, it was her favourite saying – it's never too late.

He decided to go and see May tomorrow. It was the least he could do.

20

May

Sunday was a fresh, spring-like day. James rang May around lunchtime. He was feeling more cheerful and even a little hopeful, and May answered the call really quickly, which was a good sign, he was sure.

'Jim!' she exclaimed when she heard his voice. She sounded really pleased to hear from him.

'May, how are you?' he asked. 'Can I come round and see you some time today, if you haven't got other plans?'

'I never have plans these days, Jim,' she said quietly, 'and you're very welcome to come over at any time.'

'One o'clock OK?' he asked.

'Sure. Fine with me. Look forward to seeing you later then,' she said, and hung up.

* * *

Lisa had been pleased when he'd told her where he was going and he set off feeling very positive. The traffic was fairly quiet and he arrived shortly before one o'clock. May must have seen him coming because she appeared at the door before he had even left the car.

They hugged each other on the doorstep and then she ushered him into the lounge. They had tea and biscuits and chatted to each other easily for a while. Then James told her how sorry he was about what had happened with Jack. She gave him a wary look.

'I hope you haven't come here to fight his corner, Jim,' she warned him.

'Not at all, May,' he said, shaking his head. 'I'm totally on your side in all of this. I'd have been surprised if you'd reacted any other way.'

'But Jack's your friend, Jim, you must feel sorry for him to some extent.'

She sat back and folded her arms in a rather defensive way, waiting for him to put Jack's side of the story.

He shrugged his shoulders.

'You and I go back even further than me and Jack. I suppose I might feel more sorry for him if he'd told me about it, May. I'm angry with him, not just for keeping you in the dark but for not confiding in me, either. I've been his best friend all these years and he's never said a word. All these times I've talked about Lisa while she was growing up and he never once showed any sign of telling me about his own kids. I've tried thinking back and I can't think of any time when he came anywhere close to confiding in me. Maybe because of my connection with you, but still … I feel like I didn't really know him. As if he's made a fool of me in some way, like he didn't really trust me, you know?' He looked at her enquiringly.

'I suppose that's selfish of me, but I can't help it. I know it's nothing compared to what he's done to you, but it's how I feel.'

She smiled and nodded. He really did understand something of what she was feeling. Maybe she'd been a fool to give him up for Jack all those years ago. She had always known James was the better man, more steady and reliable. But she'd fallen for Jack and that was that. She sighed.

'Love's the biggest illusion of all, isn't it, Jim?'

He started and frowned.

'Oh no, May, that's not right. I don't agree with you there. There's nothing more important than love. It can be a wonderful thing.'

She blinked at him. She'd never heard James Bolton speak like that before.

'It can be destructive, too, that's the only problem,' he said, looking at his hands thoughtfully. 'It's devastated you and it's all but destroyed Jack—'

'Oh here we go – I knew you were here for him. I knew it.' She pursed her lips and looked away from him. 'Now you'll start telling me I shouldn't have drawn away from him all those years ago, that he was starved of sex and affection and it's my own fault he went with Julia,' she said bitterly.

'I don't think that at all,' said James. 'I'm just worried about him. His health, I mean. He's going into a decline.'

'Huh, that *will* be right!' she spat out. 'Jack Forrest – a decline. Yeah right!' She laughed harshly. 'You must think I'm soft, Jim, playing that card with me,' she said disgustedly.

'He's not the man he used to be, May. Come and see for yourself if you don't believe me,' James said, knowing there was no way she was going to agree to that, but he had to try anyway.

'May, I believe Jack to be totally in the wrong in what he's done, but there is one thing you can't take away from him. He loves you so much he can't live without you – literally.'

She glared at him. He stood up to go. He'd showed her he cared and he'd told her about the state Jack was in. What she did about it, if anything, was up to her. She showed him to the door silently.

'He won't get over this, May. He's quite ill, you know,' he told her worriedly.

'You can't possibly expect me to forgive him, Jim. It's too much. It's not the affair that makes it impossible. He had children with her – kids he never even mentioned to me!' She stopped speaking in exasperation and held the door open pointedly.

'Because he was terrified of losing you, May, not because he wanted to deceive you. He knew how you'd react, and he wasn't wrong about that, was he?'

'Yes he was wrong, Jim, for your information. I feel like this because it's too late. Too damn late.' She took a deep, shaky breath.

'I'd have brought those kids up as our own if he'd told me about them at the time.'

James looked at her. He was shocked and not entirely sure he believed her. She started speaking again.

'Sure I'd have been mad – mad as hell, to begin with, but I'd have come round. They're his children and I know Julia's never wanted kids. If he'd told me about them I'd have raised them. I would, I'd have brought them up, Jim. We'd have been a family, a proper family. I'd have loved them as if they were my own.' Her voice broke.

'That's what I can't forgive him for, Jim. He took that chance away from me and we can't ever get it back now. He used to sit and talk about adoption and fostering with me and all the time ...' She couldn't go on.

'May, I don't blame you. Believe me, I don't. I understand,' he said sadly. After a moment he spoke again, tentatively.

'I don't suppose you'd want to meet them now – Jack's son and daughter?'

She raised her chin.

'No. I thought I was his life, Jim. I thought we meant everything to each other. I thought it was me and him against the world. What a fool! I'm mad at Jack and I resent his kids like hell. I'm not proud of that but it's how I feel.'

He gave up and stepped outside.

'OK, May. If you need anything or you just want to go out and let your hair down, let me know,' he told her. She nodded.

'Thanks, Jim, I might just take you up on that.' She closed the door and he left, feeling even more sorry for her than he had when he'd arrived.

Well, at least I tried, he thought. *I didn't console her much and there's no chance of her and Jack getting back together, or even of her coming to see him, but at least she knows I'm here for her.* He knew Jack and May needed each other. He was sure neither of them would ever have any happiness living apart from each other, and although there was no logical connection, he knew, deep in his heart, that while the two of them stayed apart, there was no way forward for himself and Lynsey.

21

James and May

On Monday morning James was extremely busy, because he was still doing Jack's work as well as his own, but he just *had* to speak to Lynsey. From time to time he looked up to gaze at her. She looked tired and drawn, and was noticeably losing weight; but on the plus side, her hair had grown a little longer and the black tint was gradually washing out of it. He found it hard to keep his eyes off her. She was slowly turning into the girl in the picture. He had been totally smitten with her even when she had the severe hairstyle and the heavy make-up and he'd thought she was a blatant gold-digger, but now he was simply besotted, there was no denying it. He sighed deeply as he realised how impossible the situation was, but he was determined to help her as much as he could, whether it got him any further forward with her or not.

When everyone went off for lunch she stayed at her desk. She kept lifting the phone and putting it back down again. He was sure she was still trying to get in touch with May and he walked over to her desk and sat down on the edge of it. She looked up at him and waited for him to speak.

'I've been to see May' he said, and she sat up straight.

'What did she say? Do you think she'll come and see Jack?' she asked eagerly.

'I don't think so,' he said, hating to disappoint her. 'She's very angry with him right now.'

She nodded. 'I know. I would just leave things to sort themselves out if only he wasn't in such a state. He's going to get very ill if he goes on like this. I don't know what to do.'

It occurred to him that this was probably a new experience for her, not being able to sort things out. Feeling helpless when someone you love is in trouble is one of the most frustrating and depressing things in life. He put his hand comfortingly on her shoulder.

'I'm sure Jack will come out of his depression soon and then it's only a matter of time before they get together again,' he said consolingly.

She gave him a half-smile. 'I'm not so sure, Jim. I've never seen him like this. It's like he's somebody else and not himself any more.'

'I'll stay in touch with May and try to get her to come round to him a little bit, but I can't promise anything. I can't keep harping on about it or she'll freeze me out as well and then we're stuck.'

She nodded again. 'I know, it's very difficult, isn't it? Thanks for trying anyway, Jim.' She gave him a little smile. He went back to his room thinking maybe everything wasn't so hopeless after all.

* * *

A few days later, before James had a chance to contact May again, she phoned him. He was surprised and pleased. They agreed to meet that evening.

'I'm dying to get out of the house, Jim' she told him.

'Where do you want to go?' he asked her.

'Anywhere. I don't care. I'm going stir crazy sitting in here.'

'OK, I'll book us a table somewhere then, shall I?'

'That would be lovely,' she answered.

When he hung up, he dialled Lynsey's extension.

'I'm meeting up with May again tonight,' he told her. She turned and looked at him.

'Great,' she said. 'I'll keep my fingers crossed.'

He smiled at her through his room window and put down the phone.

* * *

James and May enjoyed a very nice Italian meal together that evening and as they chatted easily to each other James felt the years slip away, back to the time when they had seen each other regularly, before he had introduced her to Jack. After a while, though, James became a little uneasy. May seemed to be enjoying his company a little too much. She kept looking into his eyes and putting her hand on his arm. And it wasn't just because she'd had a few glasses of wine. He was only too aware of how vulnerable she was right now and he was giving her the escape she needed so much.

'May, I think we should go now,' he said and she agreed reluctantly. They walked out to the car together and when they arrived at May's house she asked if he would like to come in. He said yes and they went inside.

She began to make coffee and he stood in the kitchen doorway watching her. When they sat down together in the lounge, he knew he had to say something. But it was difficult; he didn't want to alienate her and at the same time he couldn't let her think that anything was going to happen between them.

'May …' he began.

'Jim, you don't have to say anything. I know what's on your mind – Lynsey.'

He looked at her in surprise.

'Lynsey?' he said.

'You've mentioned her at least four times tonight,' she told him.

He put his head down. 'May, it isn't just that …'

'If you're going to start talking about Jack, you can leave right now,' she said firmly.

'I will if you want me to,' he said, 'but first I need to know something.' May tilted her head back and glared at him.

'May, after all Jack's done to you, do you wish him harm? I mean, do you wish him dead?' he asked her.

She frowned and said 'Of course not. How can you ask me that? Of course I don't wish him dead. I just don't want anything to do with him any more. He's hurt me too much.'

'I understand that, May, but there's something you need to know. Jack isn't dealing with this at all.' She opened her mouth to speak, but he carried on, regardless.

'I'm not saying he doesn't deserve it, I'm saying he isn't coping with it. He's ... I'm trying to think of the right way to put it. He's going under, May.'

'That isn't my problem,' she said coldly.

'No, I know it isn't. I just wanted you to be aware that he's becoming quite ill—'

'Huh!' she said, with a harsh little laugh.

'James, I'm sure you mean well, but I know Jack inside out. He's not above acting a part to get what he wants. He's manipulating you, and probably Lynsey as well. I've cut off his communication line and he's finding a way round it. That's how he operates. He's a clever man and he has no scruples when he wants something. You know that yourself.'

'That's true, May, and you're right, that is his normal self. But that's not what's happening here. Even the doctor can't get a response out of him. He's not eating, he just wants to sleep all the time. He's totally depressed and hasn't moved outside his room for weeks—'

She held up her hand.

'That's his choice, Jim. I don't want to hear any more about it. It's his problem, of his own making. I want you to go now.'

James sighed and turned to leave.

'I'm on your side, May, you know that. Call me anytime if you need me.' He smiled at her and left.

It was a flat ending to a very enjoyable evening and he really felt the anti-climax. There would be nothing but the same stalemate to report to Lynsey the next morning. If anything, May's attitude had hardened. He was flogging a dead horse trying to win her round and his worry for his friend's well-being deepened to a nagging anxiety.

* * *

The following morning, James spoke to Lynsey as soon as she came in. They went into his room and he asked her if Jack was any better.

'No, he's worse, if anything.' She looked at him hopefully. 'How was May – is she feeling a bit kinder towards him now?' she asked.

He shook his head.

'I'm afraid not, Lynsey. She doesn't want to have anything more to do with him. '

'But … didn't you tell her the state he's in?'

'Of course I did. She's hardened her heart against him. You can't blame her, really, but I had hoped she would at least contact him, come to see him even, but it's not going to happen. I'm sorry. I tried.'

He thought she was going to burst into tears, but she swallowed and blinked hard.

'What are we going to do? I don't know what else to do,' she whispered. 'I've tried talking to Jack, but he doesn't answer – he doesn't even seem to hear me. If he gets any worse I'm going to have to take time off to nurse him.'

'I'm sure the medication the doctor is giving him will lift his depression soon. Anti-depressants are very effective. And Jack'll know what to do then. He knows May best and he'll know what to do to get her back.'

She tried to smile but still looked unconvinced and went back over to her desk.

* * *

The next day she was actually smiling as she came through the door, and James felt his spirits lift immediately. He went over to speak to her.

'Is he feeling better?' he asked quietly, so that the others wouldn't hear.

'Yes, he's a little better today. He asked for a cup of coffee when I went in to see him and when I took it in to him he sat up to drink it. I know it's not much, but it's an improvement. You were right, Jim, the tablets must be starting to work!'

'Thank goodness!' he said. 'Can I come over and see him tonight?'

'Of course you can. I'm sure he'd love to see you.'

They smiled at each other and James went off to see a new client. *At least she doesn't hate me any more*, he thought hopefully.

By the time James arrived at Lynsey's flat in the evening Jack was sitting in the lounge absently looking at the television. He looked very thin and pale, but there was an alertness in his eyes that hadn't been there before. He seemed pleased to see James.

James tried to avoid talking about May, but it was impossible. Jack just nodded his head in acceptance when James said she wasn't about to come calling on him.

'That's all right, Jim' he said. 'I'll be better soon and then I can go see her myself!' He seemed hopeful, although he was still very weak physically, and by the time James left he was sure that Jack would continue to feel better now.

* * *

James was right, as it turned out. Jack's health improved steadily during the next few weeks until he was almost restored to his full strength. But James was surprised when he showed no sign of wanting to come back to work again. All he talked about was May. He was obsessed with getting her back. James didn't argue with him because he realised it was the only thing keeping him going. He didn't want him getting sick again, so he said nothing. But he knew there was no easy solution on the horizon.

May had no intention of reconciling with her husband; she was adamant about that. She had called James several times in the last few weeks and he had taken her out a couple of evenings because she didn't seem to have any other friends. Her marriage to Jack had been her whole life. The only friends she had were those she'd met through Jack. She didn't want to be around them because they reminded her of him and asked about him all the time, and she was avoiding her in-laws for the same reason.

While he was with May, James had tried to steer the conversation towards Jack a few times, but every time he did so she stopped him in his tracks and he eventually gave up trying. He settled for just enjoying her company and hoping he could eventually act as go-between for the two of them when the need arose.

22

The Wedding

Eventually, Jack's health improved enough for him to return to work, but James was concerned that he couldn't seem to concentrate properly. He kept looking away into the middle distance when James was talking to him and James was still having to do nearly all the client liaison. Jack, he was sure, was never going to be himself again until he was reunited with his wife. He was contesting the divorce and was dragging his heels as much as he could, through his lawyer, trying to buy time. James became more and more convinced he would do something drastic to win her back, but what could he do, realistically? If May had made up her mind against him, then surely that was that?

Meanwhile, James was wrestling with his own problems with his divorce from Gina and had begun to feel he would never be free of her. She was being quite unreasonable about the financial side of things. If he gave her everything she was asking for, he would be bankrupt – permanently! She'd even demanded that he sell his car! *There's no fear of that*, he assured himself. It was shaping up to be a long, bitter wrangle.

The days sped by towards summer. Life carried on in the same vein, with Jack obsessed with trying to win May back, James and May seeing each other on a friendly basis, and James and Lynsey on better terms than ever. John and Marcia were busily planning their wedding, which was to take place in June, shortly before their child was due to be born. It was to be a civil ceremony at the Hamilton Register Office, followed by a reception in the Avonbridge Hotel.

Jack had offered to pay for the whole thing so that it could happen sooner rather than later. John, initially, was not happy about this at all, but had agreed to it for Marcia's sake. It would have taken them a couple of years, at least, to save up for it on their own, especially with a little child to support. Jack had also suggested that they could afford a more salubrious venue, but Marcia was adamant that it should take place in Cadzow Street, as that was where she and John had met each other. In any case, she pointed out, the Cadzow Street Register Office had been recently refurbished and would be a fresh and pleasant place to hold the ceremony.

There was always method in Jack's madness, and James slowly began to realise that the upcoming wedding meant as much to him as it did to the bride and groom. James knew why – Jack was aware of James's friendship with May and had encouraged him to invite her to be his partner at the wedding service and the reception.

At first James had been sure she wouldn't accept the invitation, given how she felt about Jack's children, but he was wrong. Predictably, she'd turned him down at first, but then she'd rung to say she had changed her mind. She said she wanted to show Jack once and for all that things were over between them. Jack intended to make the most of the opportunity to talk her round, and James hoped he wouldn't spoil the day for John and Marcia by causing a scene. But his obsession wouldn't come to that, James was sure. He wouldn't ruin his son's wedding day. James and Lynsey had many an intimate, friendly conversation on this subject as the day approached and he felt that they had drawn closer together because of their shared anxieties.

* * *

June 15th dawned bright and beautiful and the ceremony went very smoothly. Everyone was smiling and taking photographs and Marcia looked radiant in a long cream dress edged with pearl beading. It had a little bolero, which, although short, camouflaged her bulging stomach. In fact, from the front, it was hard to tell she was even pregnant! Lynsey was full of happiness for them both and felt quite weepy as she watched them make their vows to each other. She hadn't felt like eating any breakfast, which was unusual for her, and felt a little giddy and light-headed as she stood up to join in the hymn singing. Out of the corner of her eye she could see James Bolton looking at her and she longed to turn and look into his eyes, sharing the moment with him. But she didn't, she just looked straight ahead instead. *In any case*, she told herself, *I'm with Nick now and James is still married to Gina.*

He had stopped seeing Maisie, who was now going out with a sailor, but he was getting very friendly with May, and Lynsey wasn't at all sure she liked that arrangement. They had once been lovers, after all, hadn't they? They were still going out together even though Jack was much better now and able to fight his own corner. Lynsey turned to look at Jack, who was looking rather handsome, although still a little on the thin side, but he wasn't aware of her gaze. He was staring fixedly at the back of May's head as she stood beside James watching the proceedings.

When the formalities were completed, everyone left the building and piled into the two large coaches Jack had hired for the day to take the guests to the Hotel. He followed in his own car, parking it near the edge of the sloping car park. He didn't want anything to hold him back when it was time to leave. He hoped to have May by his side again by then, if all went well.

The reception also went very smoothly, until it was time for the speeches. John's speech and that of the Best Man were fairly short but very funny, and everyone's mood had become quite mellow. Then it was Jack's turn. He was sitting at the top table with his parents and John, Marcia and Lynsey, and he made a very moving speech, which ended with him saying that he hoped that John and Marcia would be as happy as he had been in his own marriage. The silence in the room deepened perceptibly and Jack sat down again, satisfied he had said all he wanted to say. May was looking at him. She knew that was not the end of it. She stood up to go to the Ladies. She glared accusingly at Jack's parents, and then looked directly in front of her as she walked past their table, making sure she did not make eye contact with Jack.

There was a Ladies downstairs beside the Function Hall, but she went to the one upstairs, hoping that it would be a little quieter and she could get away from the crowds. She was right, it *was* quieter upstairs. She was not surprised, however, when she emerged from the Ladies to find Jack standing waiting for her. She tried to push past him, pursing her lips in annoyance.

'This is pointless, Jack,' she said in an irritated voice. 'There's no more to say.' He had taken hold of her arm. She tried to pull away, but he kept hold of her.

'Well, *I* have a lot more to say,' he told her.

She sighed in exasperation. 'Right, let's get it over with then,' she said defiantly.

'You know we're going to get back together in the end, May, once you're done punishing me.'

'I don't think I could ever punish you enough for what you've done, Jack,' she told him. 'And you're wrong about us getting back together. It would just be a farce – like the rest of our marriage.'

Jack sighed heavily.

'Will you at least think about it?' I won't give up until we're back together again,' he told her. He was trying not to get angry, but desperation was making him reckless.

'Don't hold your breath waiting!' she hissed at him, turning to go back downstairs. He blocked her way, begging her to give him another chance.

At that moment James came up the stairs looking for May.

'What's going on?' he asked, seeing their angry faces. May pushed past Jack.

'You can go to hell, Jack,' she said, just as Lynsey joined the three of them, having heard the commotion from downstairs.

'Leave May alone, Jack,' James said protectively.

'It's got nothing to do with you!' Jack answered. Then he screwed up his eyes at his friend. 'Or has it? Are you the reason she doesn't want me back? First my daughter and now my wife! I thought you were on my side, and all the time you've been—'

'That's enough!' said James, but by this time Lynsey was looking at him in disgust.

'There's nothing going on between me and May. That's rubbish! Tell him, May,' he pleaded, looking at her for back-up.

May stood with her arms folded across her chest and refused to say anything. Jack swung back his arm and his fist connected with James's jaw in a hefty blow that made him fall to his knees, bending his head in pain. By the time James had recovered he looked up to find that only May was still with him. He couldn't see Lynsey, but felt sure he had heard the door of the Ladies bang shut. She obviously believed what May had implied by her silence, or she wouldn't have left him alone after Jack had hit him. He was very angry. He rubbed his sore jaw and turned accusingly towards May to give her a piece of his mind.

No one was as upset as Jack, however, as he stormed out of the hotel door, seething. *So much for quietly talking her round*, he thought. There was no point in staying now. John and Marcia would be leaving to go on honeymoon soon and he was too angry to stand and gaily wave them off. He marched angrily across the forecourt, got into his car and winced as he pulled the door closed and heard it bang. That made him even angrier. The tyres screeched as he sped off. He hoped that a drive along the country lanes would settle him down and help him unwind. His heart was hammering and he was sweating. He tried to relax, but it wasn't working. Every time he thought about James and May together he felt as if he would explode with jealousy and rage.

He was too worked up to go back to the flat and sit alone, so he headed off in the opposite direction, towards Lanark. He sped along the narrow, twisting, hilly roads without even being aware of the picturesque views and the orange glow of the dazzling sunshine.

As he approached a particularly steep hill with a hairpin bend at the bottom, he felt a little calmer. But he was still going too fast, really. He smiled sadly to himself as a child's voice came into his head. It was Lynsey saying, 'Daddy, please don't go so fast!', as she had done so often throughout the years. Unexpected tears blurred his eyes and he blinked to clear his vision. He had never regretted anything in his life, and he would never regret having had the twins, whether he and May got back together again or not.

He knew that he really should slow down. A chill ran right down his spine as he suddenly realised he'd been in such an emotional state he'd forgotten to fasten his seatbelt. He eased up on the accelerator, but not quite quickly enough. As he rounded the bend he came face to face with an oncoming large white Transit van, which was right in the centre of the road, overtaking in the middle of the bend, and he had to veer sharply to the left to avoid a head-on collision. The wheels skidded and he fought to regain control, but it was too late. His car connected with the crash barrier at high speed and although this straightened the car's path again, he soon started suffering the effects of the impact. He experienced a sense of unreality and detachment, as if everything that was happening was just a dream. It seemed to him that the car was now moving along at speed without him. It veered off to the left just as the crash barrier came to an end and all he could see through the windscreen was grass and sky. Fate had taken control and Jack Forrest, if only for a few seconds, at last learned the meaning of regret.

23

Dark Days

When she couldn't find Jack anywhere in the Function Room, Lynsey kept asking the other guests if they had seen him. She thought he must have gone home when he wasn't even there to wave John and Marcia off, and then she began to worry. He wasn't answering his phone and hadn't replied to her text. It wasn't like him to go off in a huff.

James and May had left the reception early, not long after the argument with Jack, and Lynsey wasn't sorry to see them go. She couldn't bear to look at them. *Why do things like this always blow up at weddings?* she wondered. She didn't stay much longer herself, as she had no heart for it once John and Marcia had left. Nick did his best to cheer her up, but he soon got tired of that and went over to the bar to talk to Tim. Lynsey knew she was being a wet blanket, so she finished her drink and told Nick she was leaving early. He just nodded and said he'd see her later. She called a cab and left.

The cab dropped her off at her little flat and she called out 'Dad!' as she came in the door. The answer-phone was flashing a message and she played it as she took off her coat and shoes. It was James, telling her that Jack had been in a crash and asking her to ring the hospital straight away. She stood stock still for a moment, then rang Directory Enquiries and asked them to connect her with the hospital Accident and Emergency number.

When she said she was his daughter the nurse told her that he was still unconscious and had possibly sustained a spinal injury. She said she would come to the hospital straight away. She put the receiver down and stood for some minutes trying to collect her wits, then she grabbed her bag and coat and ran out of the door again.

She felt numb, but decided that that was for the best as she set off again in her car. She forced herself to concentrate on the road. One serious accident was quite enough for one day. She ran into A & E and was told that Jack was now in Intensive Care. When she went along there she saw James, anxiously pacing up and down, and May, who was sitting quietly in a chair, looking dazed. She had asked him to come in for a coffee after they'd left the reception and that's when the call had come from the hospital. They'd called her because, although he was living with Lynsey now, May was still officially his next of kin and his Driving Licence carried the Bothwell address.

She ran over to James. 'How is he? Is he going to be all right?' she asked anxiously.

He shook his head.

'They can't say for definite. He's still "serious" – that's all they can tell us.'

'I'm going to ring John,' Lynsey said. She went over to the payphone and dialled him. He answered straight away, sounding distracted. You don't expect any calls when you're headed off on your honeymoon! Lynsey explained what had happened and she heard him speaking to Marcia. He said they were turning round and would be coming straight to the hospital.

'I don't know if I've done the right thing,' she said to James, biting her lip. 'Should I have let them go away and not told them?' she asked him.

'No, you were right to let them know, then it's up to them what they do about it. If you didn't let them know and anything happened …'

She nodded miserably, taking a seat opposite May. It was going to be a long night.

* * *

John and Marcia arrived about an hour later. By that time, James was glad to see John, too. There was so much tension between Lynsey and May that he didn't know what to do to ease things between them. He had gone back and forward to the machine to get cups of coffee, but nothing seemed to be helping. John came straight over to Lynsey and they hugged each other tearfully.

'How is he, Lynsey? And what the hell happened anyway?' he demanded.

James answered him. 'We only know what the other driver told the hospital, that Jack was driving too fast and lost control of the car on a tight bend. That really bad one, you know, heading towards Lanark—'

'Yes, I know.' John nodded, frowning. 'What the hell was he doing heading for Lanark anyway? 'Is he going to be OK? What have they said?'

'We don't know yet, John,' Lynsey told him.

'What about the other driver?'

'Just shock. No physical injuries, apparently,' James told him. 'The Police seem to think it was more his fault than Jack's', because he was overtaking on a bend.'

John shook his head in consternation.

May closed her eyes and seemed to be meditating. Just then the doctor came over to them and they all stood up, except for May. He told them that Jack was in a coma and there was no way of telling how long he would stay unconscious. It would be some time before they could assess his spinal injury, and in the meantime his condition was still critical. Lynsey began to cry and John and Marcia comforted her. James stood by, feeling helpless. May stood up and told the doctor she wanted to sit with Jack. It wasn't that she was desperate to be by his side, she told herself, but Lynsey and John's obvious distress was affecting her and she felt she just had to get away from them for a while.

The doctor said it shouldn't be a problem, as Jack was unconscious anyway, so he showed her over to his bed and she took a seat beside him. The doctor left and she was glad to be alone with her husband. Although she felt guilty admitting it, she still couldn't accept the fact that Jack was as important to Lynsey and John as he was to her. She had always thought of him as belonging to her alone and she was still a little jealous of his closeness with them. She looked at him lying there, bruised and broken, and wondered how, or even if, he would come out of this. She remembered his arrogance earlier on and how irritated she had felt. Now she wondered if he would ever be arrogant again. He would survive, she was quite sure of that, but he would never be the man he used to be.

All sorts of dreadful possibilities chased themselves around in her mind. He could have amnesia or other brain damage, or his spinal injury could leave him paralysed. As she sat there quietly, she realised how much help he was going to need when he began to recover from this, and she wanted to be the one to help him. It wasn't that she had forgiven him for what he had done in the past, it was just that he was going to need help and that would be a new experience for Jack Forrest.

You don't deserve this, Jack, she thought, *and you don't deserve to be abandoned either.* She sighed in acceptance and felt a certain calm descend on her spirits. She would be everything to Jack again and he would be the focus of her world again, too. She forgot all about James, Lynsey and John. She could allow herself to relent towards Jack now because of his situation. It meant that no one would think she had caved in too easily, including Jack. What had happened to him was dreadful, but also, in a strange way, she felt that Fate had given her husband back to her.

Further along the IC ward, the others had settled down since May went to sit with Jack. James sat a little apart from the others, who were quieter and slightly more hopeful than they had been earlier. Lynsey was calmer now that May was with Jack, as she felt this could only be a good thing and that maybe Jack would somehow know she was there with him. John and Marcia had decided that if he remained at risk they would postpone their holiday, but would still try to go away before the baby was born. It was unthinkable that Jack would die, that he wouldn't even see his first grandchild.

James was worried sick about his friend and was considering the possibility that maybe Jack had already given up and that this was what had caused the accident, although he didn't want to believe that. He was also very much afraid that Lynsey would hold him partially responsible. She had seemed to totally believe what May had led her to believe in the hotel about herself and James being an item. Things would come right in the end, though, wouldn't they? May would be bound to set Lynsey straight as soon as Jack was out of danger. He had to try to think positively – they all had to do that now, for Jack's sake and their own.

They all settled down to wait throughout what would undoubtedly be a very long night, each of them wrapped up in their own troubles and anxieties.

24 Deadlock

At around 1.00 am the busy IC ward had quietened a little, apart from the occasional beeping of the monitoring machines. John had sent Marcia home in a taxi, as he didn't want to put her or the baby at risk by letting her get over-tired. The rest of them were beginning to nod off, but no one wanted to leave in case anything happened. May was still sitting in the chair beside Jack's bed and she was beginning to doze, too. At regular intervals, the nurse would come over to Jack's bed to check on him.

The peace was suddenly shattered when the machinery Jack was hooked up to began to sound an alarm. Everyone jolted awake and May tightened her hold on Jack's hand, hardly daring to breathe. The nurse came in swiftly and looked at the patient and the monitor. She went to find assistance and get the 'crash' trolley. She came back very quickly, with another nurse and the trolley.

'The doctor's on his way,' she told May in a soothing voice. 'Could you move away from the bed now, please?'

When the doctor arrived May went over to join the others. Through the vision panel they watched the medical team trying to resuscitate Jack. It seemed like a long time before the doctor came to speak to them again. They all stood up and he told them Jack's condition had stabilised and he was out of danger. They were all very relieved. Lynsey sat back down and put her hands over her face and John gave her a squeeze. May dabbed at her eyes and asked if she could sit with him again. The doctor said she could but warned her he may not regain consciousness for some time. She went over to sit beside him and the nurse told the others that now he was out of danger the best thing they could do was to go home and get some sleep.

After John and Lynsey had left, James went over to ask May if she needed him to stay. She turned to him and said that she was fine and that if she needed to get home she would call a taxi.

'I'm glad he's going to be OK,' he said. She smiled and turned back towards Jack.

James left, feeling sure that Jack and May would find each other again now. He was aware of driving more carefully than usual on his way home.

* * *

The next morning was Sunday and Lynsey slept later than she had intended. She felt very tired. She always seemed to feel tired these days. Yesterday had been exhausting and she felt emotionally drained, too. She was very relieved that Jack was out of danger now, and that his accident had brought May to his side again, but having had time to think about things overnight, she was very angry and disappointed by James's behaviour. Jack's state of mind before the crash, it seemed to her, was a direct result of James and May going out together when Jack was so desperate for a reconciliation. If she had needed any confirmation that her judgement was flawed where James Bolton was concerned, May had done that at the hotel yesterday. She didn't blame May as much as she did James because Jack had hurt May so much that she was bound to have been feeling very let-down and lonely.

Lynsey decided she would have nothing more to do with James, other than at work, but she wished that decision didn't make her feel so unhappy. She could feel depression settling on her spirits like a dark cloud as she drove off to the hospital.

When she spoke to the IC nurse, she was told that her father was no longer there but had been moved to an individual room on one of the wards. She hurried along the corridor, getting herself lost a couple of times before she got there. When she arrived, the nurse told her May had gone home for some rest and that Jack's condition remained the same. He was stable but still unconscious. She was allowed in to see him and she entered his room softly, tiptoeing across the polished floor, then she realised that was a silly thing to do, as waking him up could hardly be a bad thing!

There were a couple of seats on either side of his bed and she sat down on the one nearest him. She was almost afraid to look at him. He didn't look like himself, lying there, oblivious to everything. He looked like a corpse that was breathing, she thought, and her eyes filled with tears for him. She reached out and took his hand in hers, squeezing it gently. It had been bad enough when he was depressed and sleeping all the time; now his situation was much, much worse. She sent up a silent prayer that his coma would be short-lived and not drag on and on, as so often happens in cases of severe trauma. She tried to cheer herself up by telling herself that at least May would be there for him now, and that would make all the difference to him, if he ever woke up again to realise it!

She had been sitting there for some time when James and May arrived together. Seeing them together made her resentful all over again.

'Is he any better?' May asked.

'No, just the same,' she answered stiffly, turning back to Jack so that she wouldn't have to look at James. She asked May if she wanted to sit nearer to Jack and she nodded. Lynsey stood up to give up her seat and said she was going to get a cup of coffee. As she left the room she could hear James walking behind her, following her into the corridor.

'Lynsey, have you got a minute?' he asked, and she turned round to face him, her eyes steely and her jaw set.

'I don't want to hear it,' she said coldly.

'What May did yesterday – I know she refused to deny that we were an item, probably to annoy Jack, but there is nothing going on between us. I swear to you.'

'Nothing to do with me,' she said tartly. 'As long as you can sleep at night.' She looked straight at him, her meaning clear. 'Anyway, I've got more on my mind than this right now.'

She went off down the corridor to the coffee machine. He came up behind her as she lifted her coffee out, and spoke to her back.

'You accused me before of thinking the worst of you without giving you a chance to explain. Now you're doing the same thing to me,' he challenged her, determined to set the record straight.

She answered him through clenched teeth.

'You have the nerve to stand there as if you're totally innocent! I believed you when you said you were trying to talk May round, trying to heal the breach with Jack. And all the time you were making a move on her. No wonder Jack was in despair. No wonder he came off the road—'

'Lynsey, that's not fair. I—' He didn't get any further. He turned as the nurse appeared beside them and spoke to Lynsey.

'Miss Robson, your father's awake!'

Lynsey dumped her coffee down on a nearby table and hurried off along the corridor back to Jack's room, with James close behind her. He was not allowed to see Jack, however, as the doctor had decreed that only family members should be by his bedside at that time, so as not to tire him out. James was advised to go back home, as Jack would need to rest, and when he wasn't resting, his family would take priority as visitors. Just as he was wondering whether to go or stay, John and Marcia arrived, and James told them Jack was awake and that he was going off home now, so he wouldn't be in the way. They hardly even noticed him leaving.

He rang the hospital later that day, to be told that Jack was still very weak but was making good progress. He found that easy to believe, as he now had his wife and family by his side, and that would give him the strength to get better. He asked the nurse to tell Jack he'd called and then hung up. He spent the rest of that day trying to feel positive about Jack's recovery, but he couldn't stop brooding over his argument with Lynsey. She didn't believe him and he couldn't blame her. It was exasperating, but he wasn't going to just let it drop. He wanted her to know the truth, even if it didn't bring them any closer together.

* * *

As James sat in his room at Forrest & Bolton just before 9 o'clock the next day, he wondered whether Lynsey would come in to work or not, and if she would speak to him if she did. She came running through the door a moment later, looking pale and tired and harassed. He gave her a few moments to settle herself and then went over to ask her about Jack.

'He's still very weak, and he's still got that brace thing round his neck. He's got to have some tests on his back. They still think his spine could be damaged,' she told him, frowning worriedly.

'Well, give him my best when you see him, won't you? I won't come in to visit him till he's stronger. I'm sure he just wants his family around him right now.' He gave her a little smile and went back to his room. He deliberately hadn't mentioned May. He didn't want to antagonise her again. She didn't answer him, just nodded her head and turned away. She frowned as he walked away from her.

He was a puzzle to her – one minute he was behaving despicably and the next, he was being considerate and supportive! It was too much for her to think about with everything else that was happening, but she didn't like being undecided about anyone, especially James. Her judgement seemed to desert her where he was concerned because she wanted to think well of him. She made a mental note to ask May what had really happened between them as soon as Jack was better.

Meanwhile, James was in despair. He felt as though everything in his life was falling apart. For one thing, he missed Lisa a great deal. She was engrossed in her new life and friends, including her new boyfriend, and he rarely heard from her. His marriage was over and he didn't even know when he would be free or where he was going to live now. He was worried about Jack, and also about how he himself would cope in the office, as obviously Jack would not be back at work for some time.

Lynsey wasn't saying much because she was preoccupied with her father's recovery, but he knew she still didn't trust him. He had been sure things would improve between them once Jack and May had made their peace with each other, but because of the way it had come about, their relationship had gotten worse instead of better. *One step forward and two steps back, that's how it seems to go with us*, he thought. He put his head down and got on with his work, his heart like a lump of lead in his chest. He would try to have a talk with her later in the day, he decided. He couldn't go on like this.

* * *

As Lynsey was leaving the office that evening, James caught up with her in the car park.

'Lynsey, can I have a word?' he asked. He sounded anxious and distracted and she stopped and waited for him to speak.

'Could we go somewhere for a drink, or just go for a walk or something?' he asked.

She hesitated. 'I'm going to see Dad.'

'It won't take long, I promise.'

'OK then,' she said, 'we can walk around the block if you want.'

They set off down the street and James suddenly couldn't decide where to start, how to approach things with her. There was a bench a little further along and they both sat down when they came to it, each of them staring straight ahead.

'Do you still blame me for what happened to your father?' James asked her directly.

'Whether you and May were an item or not, he thought you were,' she said, still staring ahead.

'I was trying to help, Lynsey. I thought I could bring them together again if I stayed friendly with both of them.'

'And why would you be so keen to do that? Out of the goodness of your heart, I suppose? You used to go out with May yourself. Don't tell me it never crossed your mind that you could get back with her again if you cut Jack out of the picture.'

He looked directly at her.

'Lynsey, that wasn't what I intended at all. They love each other, they've been together a long time and they belong together. I envy what they've got, but I would never, *never* try to come between them. I don't know what else I can say. I like May very much, but I'm not interested in her as a partner. And even if I was, I wouldn't do that to Jack. Please believe me, Lynsey.' He held his breath as he waited for her to answer.

'I don't know what to believe any more,' Lynsey said. 'You and Jack have that in common, you always know how to get round people,' she said, giving him a hard stare. 'You were very convincing in your apologies the night you stayed with me, too, as I remember, and everything you said was a load of rubbish!'

He swallowed and cringed inside. *It's no use*, he thought, *this is always going to come between us. She doesn't want to know me.* She stood up and walked away from him.

'Just leave me alone from now on, I can't be bothered with this,' she said dismissively, over her shoulder.

He felt dejected. He'd been so sure things would improve between the two of them once Jack and May got together again, but obviously he'd been wrong. He gazed after her, tears welling in his eyes. He was sure now that it was over for good. The plain truth was that, because of his initial attitude towards her and all the things that had gone wrong between them since, he'd lost her trust and he didn't know of any way to ever get it back again.

25

Healing Time

During what was left of the summer, John and Marcia eventually had their honeymoon in Kefalonia, Lynsey and James spoke to each other very rarely, and Jack made a certain amount of progress in his recovery. He had been so happy when he'd regained consciousness that day and had seen May sitting beside him, holding his hand and willing him to be all right! Even though he was exhausted and in quite a bit of pain, he'd known that everything would work out now. They had talked and talked, as soon as he had gained a little strength, and things were almost as good between them as they had been before Julia dropped her bombshell.

He couldn't remember anything about the accident at all. He recalled driving along approaching a bad bend and seeing a van coming towards him, but nothing after that until he woke up in hospital. He didn't mind, as he didn't want to remember it anyway. However, he was still confined to bed and only able to move the top half of his body. His doctors were not forthcoming about his spinal injuries, possibly because they didn't know the full prognosis themselves yet.

As the weeks passed, however, Jack became increasingly fractious because he couldn't get out of bed and could do very little for himself, and he didn't want May to stay with him just because she felt sorry for him. He didn't need anyone's pity, especially hers. One evening, when May came in at visiting time, he was more out of sorts than usual and she asked him what was wrong.

'Oh I don't know,' he said sarcastically. 'A young doctor who looks about twelve years old just told me I'm probably never going to walk again, but apart from that everything's fine!'

She looked at him levelly.

'We'll get through this together, Jack. Financially, you don't need to work any longer and I'll always be here to look after you—'

'What, and push me about in my wheelchair? That sounds wonderful!' he spat out.

She took a deep breath.

'They haven't said you *definitely* won't walk again,' she said quietly.

'I don't want you with me out of pity,' he said shakily.

'Beggars can't be choosers,' she answered, watching his jaw tighten in annoyance.

Then she smiled. She had made him angry and that was better than being miserable.

'I can walk away from you if that's what you want,' she told him, standing up and lifting her bag.

'Oh yes, go on, rub it in. You can walk away and I can't!'

She started to leave.

'OK, you win, I get the message,' he said, closing his eyes in defeat, his heart thumping heavily. 'There's worse things than being a cripple – there's being a cripple on your own,' he said, glaring at her petulantly.

'And,' she added, walking back and sitting down again, 'I've got a captive audience, so we're playing *my* game for a change!'

For a moment he stared at her in disbelief, wondering how she could be so cruel. *Is she getting her own back on me for hurting her?* he wondered. Then he realised she wouldn't speak to him like that if she only felt pity for him. She was right. Even if he *was* going to be crippled, there was something in his life that made his physical condition bearable, and he would never let himself forget that again. It reminded him of the time when, as a small child, he'd had a tooth pulled at the dentist and afterwards his mother had given him a bag of his favourite sweets to console him. He felt himself starting to smile, albeit reluctantly, and he sat back and listened to May talking to him. At least he let her think that he was listening – what he was actually doing was planning his strategy for the future. He would be in control again, just as he always was. No matter what it took. He had the money and now he had the incentive. He would get the best doctors, surgeons, physio-therapists, whatever it took. *There'll be no Disabled cars for me*, he resolved, *I'm going to beat this!*

* * *

While Jack was coming to terms with his pain that day, Marcia was experiencing quite a different kind of pain. She and John had returned from honeymoon two days previously and had been out shopping for most of the day. They were both pottering around in the kitchen preparing the evening meal. He was really getting on her nerves today, which was unusual. In fact, everything was getting on her nerves today! Her bump was large and heavy now and she had definitely overdone things by walking too much. After all, she was due in two weeks' time. Her back was aching so much she told John to shut up and went off into the lounge to sit down for a while. John came in from the kitchen looking aggrieved.

'What have I said now?' he asked, then stood still as he took in her white, strained face. He walked over to her and touched her shoulder. 'You're not in labour, are you?' he asked in concern.

'No, I've just got a really sore back,' she answered. He felt an odd mixture of relief and disappointment.

'OK, I'll do the tea. You just sit there and relax. Probably too much walking today. Lynsey'll give me a row for not taking care of you properly.' He went back into the kitchen muttering to himself.

He was clattering about, pulling pots and pans out of the cupboard, thinking that they really must save harder and buy a proper house with bigger cupboards once the baby arrived, when he heard Marcia calling him. He ran back and found her with her eyes tight shut, holding her back and groaning in obvious pain. She wasn't saying anything now, and if Marcia wasn't saying anything, then she was really hurting!

'I'll call the hospital,' he said reassuringly, determined not to panic. When he had made the call, he rushed upstairs to get the little bag she had packed a couple of weeks ago, threw his jacket into the car along with it and came back for his wife. He helped her out to the car and tried not to speed on the way to the hospital, which, thankfully, wasn't too far away! By the time he'd helped her in the door, she could hardly stand up and he had to virtually carry her to the desk. The nurses came to give him a hand and they got her down to the Labour ward.

'I think she's about ready to deliver!' one of them said. 'She's been in labour for hours. Why didn't you get here earlier?' they asked him reproachfully. He blinked and stuttered.

'I didn't know,' he said stupidly, 'she said she had a sore back.'

'That's the way it happens sometimes,' he was told. He nodded dumbly as she was whisked away from him. Less than thirty minutes later he watched her give birth to their daughter.

* * *

'They're calling her Kylie,' Lynsey told everyone proudly as she announced the good news at work the next day. '6lbs, 5 ounces. Just think, I'm an auntie now!'

James listened to her and thought to himself that she would make a lovely aunt, and an even lovelier mother! He tried to pull his thoughts back to reality, but it was no use. Once that picture was in his head, there was no getting rid of it. *Get real, Jim*, he told himself, *you never really had a chance with her to begin with, even before you screwed up!*

Back in his room, he sat down at his desk to open his mail, sighing distractedly. The envelopes reminded him that he had received a letter at home that morning, which he hadn't had time to open yet. He took it out of his inside pocket and slit it open. He had known it was about the divorce, as it was obviously from his solicitor. Alex had been a friend for years, although they didn't really see much of each other these days, and he was a wizard at divorce proceedings, but Gina was demanding a ridiculous settlement and it looked like it was all going to drag on for years. He put his hand over his forehead and bent his head, closing his eyes in despair. When he looked up again, Gina was standing in front of him, as if his thoughts had conjured her up.

'You'll have to cough up in the end,' she said nastily. 'You might as well do it now, otherwise she'll be with someone else by the time you're free,' she said, tilting her head in Lynsey's direction. 'And she looks the type to want a ring on her finger before you get anything from her.'

That did it. James stood up and took her arm. He propelled her out of the building and told her never to come back. Then he returned to his room, banged the door shut and sat down at his desk, putting his head in his hands again. *Will this nightmare never end?* he wondered.

Lynsey sat very still in her seat. She was stunned, and the realities of James Bolton's marriage suddenly made more sense to her. It was quite obvious to her that the woman she had just seen must be James's wife, but she had come across her before. She shuddered as she thought back to that night a few months ago when she'd seen her and that other woman together and had escaped hurriedly from the Ladies. It was clear to her now what James had had to put up with from Gina, and why he had turned to Maisie on a long-term basis. She knew he was having difficulty extricating himself from the marriage and was also quite sure he didn't know about Gina's girlfriend.

She stood up and walked into to his room. He looked up in surprise, noticing as he did so that she wasn't looking too well.

A pile of property details and photographs lying on his desk distracted her momentarily. She knew he was looking for a new home, but these were substantial houses.

'Aren't those rather large for you – you'd be rattling around in something that size on your own. I'd have thought you'd have gone for a flat,' she commented.

He closed the file over and said curtly that he wanted a house with a garden.

'Was there something else, Lynsey?' he asked, not wanting to discuss his choice of home with her at that point.

'Was that Gina who just came to see you?' she asked.

'Yes,' he said, amazed she didn't know that already. 'Haven't you met her before?'

'Oh yes, I've met her before,' she answered pointedly, making him even more puzzled.

'I hear she's being difficult about the divorce.' she stated.

'She's being quite impossible. She's going to ruin me.'

'She can't do that, surely? She hasn't got a leg to stand on,' Lynsey said, matter-of-factly.

'How do you mean?' said James, frowning.

'You must know she bats for the other side,' she told him.

He seemed taken aback for a moment, without really being surprised. Then he said,

'Don't be ridiculous. I think I'd know something like that after eighteen years—'

'Does she have a lot of girlfriends, or just one special friend?'

'She has a best friend, Lili, but there's nothing wrong with that; so do a lot of women.' He was having a hard time believing his wife could have hidden something like that from him.

'The private eye said she wasn't seeing anyone,' he added lamely.

'Well, he was following your instructions and looking for a man, wasn't he? Sometimes you don't see what you're not looking for.' She told him about the incident in the restaurant toilet, then she walked out of his room and left him to digest the information.

He stood up and gazed out of his window with his hands in his trouser pockets, his mind in a whirl. His embarrassment, especially with Lynsey knowing the situation, was acute, and his anger towards Gina was severe. His chest heaved with anger and humiliation, but these feelings soon gave way to the sudden realisation that, although this new information would make him look foolish in the eyes of everyone he knew in the short-term, it was also his escape route. At long last, there was light at the end of the tunnel!

* * *

Gina was really surprised to see James at her door that night. She stood back to let him come in without a word.

'Decided to see sense, have you?' she said, smirking, then broke off as she noticed he was smiling. *Maybe he's going to kill me instead*, she thought, a little hysterically. Her eyes narrowed and she drew deeply on her cigarette.

'Come on then, let's see what you've got!' she taunted him, as she had done so many times over the years. She had taken pleasure in encouraging him physically and then laughing in his face when she rejected him.

'How's Lili?' he asked meaningfully.

'What's it to you?' she carped back at him, beginning to get suspicious.

'You can have the house, because it's a home for Lisa to come back to if she ever needs it, but that's it. If you try and get any more from me I'll have to have a little chat with Alex – about Lili.'

'What about her?' she hedged.

'I'm done playing your games. Take the settlement or you'll get nothing at all. Let's face it, when all's said and done, it's *you* that owes *me!*' he finished angrily.

She stubbed out her cigarette in the ashtray, taking her time to answer him.

'Took you long enough,' she said at last, giving him her usual contemptuous look. This time, however, he realised it wasn't about him personally. She had tied herself to him for financial gain, not wanting him or any other man anywhere near her. It wasn't really him she despised, it was herself. Her own lie had poisoned her mind. She knew what she had done to him over the years, psychologically, and her own guilt had made her hate the sight of him.

'Piss off then!' she hissed at him. It was her way of conceding defeat.

'Gladly,' he told her, turning towards the door. 'If I never see you again it'll be too damn soon for me.'

As he walked away, he felt the way she always made him feel – as if she'd tied a strait-jacket around him and he was struggling to pull it off. But he didn't hate her any more now that he was free of her, he didn't feel anything for her at all. As he closed the door firmly behind him, he drew in a long draught of cool, fresh air and straightened himself up. It was as if a ton weight had been lifted from his shoulders. He made up his mind to find somewhere else to stay as quickly as possible. The sooner he left this house, the better.

26

Birthday

Forrest & Bolton had employed a new receptionist to cover Marcia's Maternity Leave. Jennifer was a small, quiet girl in her early twenties, with a sweet personality and a mane of very long, naturally blonde hair, which she kept tied back tidily in a thick plait during the working day.

Right from the start, Jenny was very taken with Nick. He was always very pleasant to her, but he never flirted with her. When Tim remarked that she was nice looking, Nick replied that she was okay but she wasn't as sexy as Lynsey. He didn't seem to notice the long, lingering looks she gave him from beneath her thick, fair lashes, but Lynsey did. She gradually came to realise that Jenny had really fallen for him. Lynsey and Nick's relationship was easy and undemanding, but lately she had been feeling even more tired than usual and inclined to spend more time by herself. Nick was beginning to get a little weary of this arrangement, and although he wasn't in love with Lynsey, it annoyed him that she was being so cool towards him. Lynsey began to think that it might be best to call it a day with him, but she just couldn't be bothered with the hassle. She felt as though she couldn't really be bothered with anything, so she just let things carry on as usual.

On the last day of September, Jenny brought in a box of cakes and handed them out around the staff, explaining that it was her birthday.

'Hey, we'll have to go to the pub tonight to celebrate!' suggested Tim.

'Yeah, I think we should, Tim. Any excuse, eh!' said Nick, seeing Jenny's surprised expression. 'Well, are you up for it then, Jen?' he asked her.

'Oh, I don't know' she answered him uncertainly, blushing uncomfortably. 'It's a week night and …'

'So what?' Nick scoffed, 'a couple of drinks won't do any harm, will it?'

'OK then,' she agreed doubtfully.

Nick looked over at Lynsey.

'Count me out,' she said, shaking her head.

'Oh, come on,' he coaxed her. 'You know you want to!'

'Nick, I'm tired—'

'You're always bloody tired these days, Lynsey. Know what, you're no fun any more.'

She shrugged and carried on half-heartedly with her work.

At 5 o'clock Nick and Lynsey parted outside the building with a frosty little peck on the cheek.

'See you tomorrow,' Lynsey said and walked off slowly towards her car. Nick turned away from her and put his arms across Tim's and Jenny's shoulders as they followed the others along to the pub.

'I don't want to be out too late,' Jenny said, a little anxiously.

'Party pooper!' Nick teased her, noticing how soft her hair felt against his fingers.

When Jenny had complained earlier to Lynsey that she wasn't dressed for a night out, she'd persuaded her to let her hair flow loose so that she'd feel more glamorous. It had worked and Jenny had added a little pale pink gloss to her lips, silently cursing her neat figure and wishing that she looked more like Lynsey so that Nick would fancy her. Unknown to her, she needn't have worried, as Nick was finding it difficult to keep his eyes off her at that point in time.

The evening was fun and everyone wanted to buy her a drink for her birthday.

'I can't drink any more or I won't be able to get up for work tomorrow,' she told Nick when they'd been in the pub for about three hours.

'Do you want to call it a day then?' he asked her. 'We could share a taxi if you want.'

She nodded and Nick used his mobile to ring for one. Jenny, Nick and Tim all got into the cab when it arrived, and they dropped Tim off first. He winked at Nick as he got out, but he pretended not to notice.

When they arrived at Jenny's place she asked Nick if he'd like to come in for a coffee and he only hesitated for a second before he agreed. They squabbled good-naturedly over who should pay for the cab and then went inside together, laughing and more than a little tipsy.

Jenny pottered about in the tiny kitchenette area making the coffee, and then they went into the main part of her little bed-sit to drink it. They chatted easily at first, but as they finished their drinks they both fell silent and Nick said he'd better be going. Jenny bit her lip to stop herself from asking him to stay. They both stood up and Nick came over to her and took her mug from her hand. Their hands touched and attraction flared between them. He put the mugs down on the coffee table and took both of her hands in his own.

He thought about Lynsey, but that didn't help, as he could picture her tired face and hear her bored voice, and it just made Jennifer seem even more appealing. Her large, doe-like eyes were bright and clear and he just couldn't stop himself from kissing her. Her lips were soft and sweet and he didn't want the kiss to end. She groaned as he began to slowly kiss her face and then her neck. She drew back a little and looked up at him.

'Nick, what about Lynsey? She's my friend and she's your girlfriend!'

Nick sighed distractedly. He stopped kissing her, but being so close to her was driving him crazy and he didn't want to stop at all.

'We're not exclusive or serious or anything,' he said, feeling like a bit of a heel. She tried to move away from him, but she didn't really want him to let her go and she was glad when he kept on holding her. Suddenly he said, 'Jen, Lynsey and I are over. I wanted to tell her before I mentioned it to anyone else, but I didn't know this was going to happen.'

'It's not because of me, is it?' she asked, frowning worriedly.

'No. It's just run its course, that's all. You saw what she was like today. She's not really interested. I think she's got someone else on her mind, actually.'

She nodded. It had been hard for her to understand why Lynsey was so cool with Nick, but now that she did she was sure what was happening between them tonight wasn't going to hurt her friend. She relaxed and smiled shyly, drawing him close to her again. He drew in his breath sharply. How could he have thought she wasn't as sexy as Lynsey? Her hair was like silk, her skin was soft and smooth as a baby's and she smelt wonderful. She had a small bust, but as he slowly undid her bra and cupped her breasts he knew she had pushed all thoughts of Lynsey's lushness from his mind for ever. He almost felt as if he were sinking down into a massive tidal wave, but it wasn't an unpleasant sensation, and they held onto each other tightly and drowned in it together.

27

Kylie's Christening

Lynsey and James were standing as godparents. It was a beautiful service in a lovely old church, and the sun streamed through the stained-glass windows. James stood proudly beside Lynsey. It felt right just being there by her side. Lynsey couldn't help smiling as she looked round at everyone in their Sunday best, all keeping quiet and trying to look serious. Marcia was wearing a peach and cream outfit, which was just as well as little Kylie was bringing back some of her bottle, and it didn't show up too much against those colours! As Lynsey was rather thinner than usual, she was happily wearing a cream linen trouser suit, so they were co-ordinating well with each other for the photographs. Almost all of the men were wearing light grey suits and brightly coloured ties. Even Jack looked well, sitting smartly attired in his wheelchair, and May was standing contentedly by his side, wearing a dress and matching coat in a smooth, taupe-coloured fabric.

The others from the office all stood together, trying not to appear bored and looking forward to the party afterwards. There were several babies and families at church that morning for the same purpose, and it was some time before the service ended and they all went back to Jack and May's house to wet the baby's head.

By the middle of the afternoon the party was in full swing. Marcia was relaxed and enjoying herself for the first time since the birth, so when little Kylie started demanding her 2 o'clock feed, May volunteered to see to her and took her off upstairs with all her paraphernalia. Lynsey went up the stairs behind her to give her a hand. She hadn't had a chance to hold the baby yet and also she wanted to speak to May in private.

While May fed the baby her milk, Lynsey was busy organising things for changing her nappy. Then she sat down.

'She's so lovely, isn't she?' she said.

'Yes, she's a real sweetie,' said May. Then she looked at Lynsey. 'I owe you an apology, Lynsey, for the way I carried on before, dropping James in it like that. There was never anything going on. You do know that, don't you? I was just trying to get back at Jack.'

The milk being finished now, May gently handed the baby over to be changed.

'I know,' Lynsey said, sighing. 'I was pretty hard on him, too, at that time, and now he's doing what I asked him to do and leaving me alone!' She smiled sadly as she cuddled Kylie for a moment and stroked her back to break her wind before changing her nappy. May knew she owed Lynsey for the way she had treated her previously, not to mention her behaviour with James.

'I don't know what went wrong between you and James,' May said, 'but I do know he's in love with you.'

Lynsey's head came up sharply.

'What makes you think that?' she asked, holding the nappy in mid-air while she waited for the answer.

'Because he told me,' said May. *Well, it's only a little fib*, she thought, *and it's in a good cause!*

Lynsey fixed the baby's nappy and then wrapped her up cosily and held her against her chest as she considered May's words, her intuition telling her that May was exaggerating when she said James was in love with her. She was trying to make up for coming between them.

Lynsey knew that deep down she had long since forgiven James for everything he had actually done and for the things she had wrongly believed he had done, but this in itself worried her a little. She was normally quite inclined to sulk and it wasn't like her to forgive so easily, but where he was concerned she just wanted things to be all right between them. She would have to be careful that he didn't start thinking he could treat her any way he liked and she would come running back to him whenever it suited him.

While Lynsey rocked Kylie off to sleep, May came downstairs to find Jack. He was surrounded by people and enjoying the attention. He had quickly noticed, since he'd been in his chair, that people would just run around doing anything he asked them, and he wasn't above deliberately using his condition to get his own way. When May asked him to do something to help Lynsey and James along, he said he would. He still felt guilty about the accusations – and the punch – he'd thrown at his friend during the reception. May had told Jack the truth about their relationship shortly after he'd regained consciousness. As soon as he'd come home from hospital James had come to see him and Jack had apologised for jumping to the wrong conclusions. James had forgiven him readily, assuring him that there were times when he'd jumped to wrong conclusions himself in the past!

Jack had a word with John, asking him if he would mediate between Lynsey and James. John nodded and agreed that James needed talking to, but he didn't mention that he had his own version of what he needed to be told!

James was standing at the large dining-room table. He wasn't bothering with any of the food; he just gazed soulfully out of the window, sipping a soft drink. John walked over to him. James looked smart in his grey suit and silvery-blue tie, but his face was tired and drawn and it had been an effort to smile for the photographs. He managed a smile for John, however.

'Lovely Christening service, John. You must be on top of the world,' he said, sipping his orange juice.

'I am,' John agreed, 'and I'm impressed with how well Jack's coping. He's even made his peace with mother again, which I didn't think was ever on the cards. I don't know if Lynsey will ever forgive her, though. She's a very understanding person, but not very forgiving when someone really hurts her, if you know what I mean.' He looked straight at James to make sure his words had hit home. 'How are you getting on with Jack's replacement?'

'Oh, fine,' James answered. Jack intended coming back to work at some point and so they had hired an experienced estate agent to help James out on a temporary basis. John looked at James and cleared his throat.

'Nick and Lyns make a nice couple, don't they?'

'Yes,' agreed James. In reality, he'd been hoping that things would have fizzled out between them by now.

'There's something I still don't understand – about you and Lynsey,' he added.

'What?' John asked, frowning.

'How come you've got different surnames?' asked James.

'Well, when mother married Tony, Lynsey wanted us all to be a proper family, so she took his name, Robson, but I decided just to stay as "Smith". I *had* hoped that Jack would acknowledge us sooner and I could change it to Forrest and carry on the family name, but it never happened,' he explained, a little edge of lingering resentment in his voice.

'Right, I see,' said James. 'You and Marcia seem to be very happy together,' he added.

'Yes we are, John replied, grinning widely. 'And don't be surprised if you're hearing wedding bells again soon,' he added cheerily, nodding over towards where Lynsey now stood chatting and laughing with Nick. John watched James's expression change, and when he was satisfied that his words had had the desired effect, he walked over to join his sister.

After everyone had said their goodbyes, James headed in Lynsey's direction to try to talk to her, but he didn't get the chance. He knew she was to be off work on holiday during the coming week and she hadn't even said goodbye to him. He hadn't thought his spirits could sink any lower, but as he watched her and Nick drive off together, they did.

Lynsey sat very quietly during the journey home, as she had a great deal on her mind. Apart from Jack still being in a wheelchair, things had worked out well for everyone else, except herself and James. She remembered what May had told her and now that James was a free man, she knew that she wanted to get to know him better and to decide for herself whether his behaviour after the Christmas dance was out of character or not. He had been very wrong about her and had jumped to conclusions when he'd seen her and Jack together. She understood how that had happened, but it was also true that she had judged him unfairly, too, with regard to his relationship with May. Given his past, he was bound to be carrying a certain amount of emotional baggage. All her instincts told her that he was basically a decent man who, so far, had had a raw deal as far as his love-life was concerned. She couldn't stop thinking about him and couldn't imagine moving away and trying to forget him, so she was prepared to take a chance on getting hurt again.

The problem was that she didn't know how to convey her change of heart to him. After the way she'd told him to stay away from her, there was no way he was going to approach her again. Also, he was somewhat older than her and therefore would probably not appreciate a woman making the first move. She had to let him know that there was no barrier between them now, but wasn't sure how to go about it. She considered several options, unsure of what to do but quite sure that she had to do *something* soon. By the time they arrived at the flat, a little plan had formed in her mind, but she would need John's help to do it and she suspected he would be more likely to sabotage it than help it along.

She was so absorbed in her thoughts that she jumped when Nick spoke to her.

'You're miles away,' he said.

'Nick ...' she began.

'Lynsey,' he interrupted her. 'I need to talk to you. About us. It's—'

The corners of her mouth curved up a little. 'Jen?' she asked.

He nodded in surprise, and she could see he was trying not to look too relieved.

'I didn't realise you knew. I hope you're not mad at me.'

'Of course not, Nick. We were only killing time with each other anyway.' She smiled at him, hoping she didn't look too relieved herself.

28

Lynsey's Condition

When Lynsey returned to work the following week, James seemed almost to be ignoring her. She had thought a great deal about him during her week off and about how to resolve the situation between them. On a visit to John and Marcia towards the end of the week, while Marcia was busy with the baby, she had gone into the kitchen to help her brother make the tea. He'd asked how she was enjoying her week off and she'd said it was fine, but that she missed the company at work. John had given her a long look then turned and busied himself at the sink.

'Nice to get a break from James, though, isn't it? He's quite snippy with you sometimes.'

'Well, he used to be,' Lynsey had agreed, 'but he's okay with me now.'

'Don't be taken in,' he'd advised. 'He's a bit of a misogynist, you know.'

'Remind me never to get on the wrong side of you, John,' she'd said, a touch of reproach in her voice. 'You're supposed to be his friend!'

'Oh, he's a great guy, don't get me wrong. He's a good mate, but as far as women are concerned, he's bad news.'

She'd frowned, feeling rather deflated. She was a bit puzzled by John's attitude. The more convinced she became that he was trying to come between her and James, for reasons best known to himself, the more inclined she was to follow her own instincts. But John's warnings had unsettled her and now she felt unsure if James was even interested in getting together with her again. She'd tried to change the subject, saying, 'The Christening was lovely.'

'Yes it was, wasn't it?' he'd agreed proudly. 'I was surprised Jim didn't bring Maisie, though, weren't you?' he'd asked innocently.

'Maisie – he finished with her ages ago,' she'd told him. 'Didn't he?'

'If you say so,' he'd replied flippantly, the implication obvious. She'd frowned and steered clear of the subject for the rest of her visit.

* * *

James hardly spoke to her that Monday and she was very busy, doggedly trying to catch up with the pile of work that had built up on her desk in her absence, but her mind was distracted and she had so little energy that she found it hard to concentrate. She decided the situation with James was going to drive her crazy and she had to resolve it one way or the other.

Nick and Jen were keeping quiet about being an item, as they wanted to give their relationship a chance to get off the ground before everyone else got to know about it, and she couldn't very well make a special point of telling James the situation, as they barely spoke to each other. But she knew she would have to sort things out soon. If he wasn't interested, it would be embarrassing, but at least then she would know where she stood.

She continued to feel unwell, although it generally seemed to ease up later in the day. In the afternoon she rang the surgery to get her test results.

'But I can't be. Are you sure?' she exclaimed, when they told her what the problem was. James was speaking to John at the time and was listening to her whilst pretending not to. He was fairly sure he knew what her test results were.

She started taking her tablets the next morning. She hadn't had any breakfast and didn't feel like eating anything during the morning, and when she stood up to get her coat at lunchtime she moved too fast and made herself feel dizzy. Then the dizziness got worse, everything seemed to get very bright and there was a funny noise in her ears. Although she had never fainted before, she knew she was going to pass out. She bent forward, but it was too late. Just as the floor rushed up towards her, she felt John's arms around her, stopping her from falling. James had seen the whole thing from his room and came hurrying over to them.

She came round very quickly to find both James and John looking at her anxiously. She felt a little silly. She should have eaten something, she realised belatedly, whether she was hungry or not.

'I'm all right, I'm okay now,' she said, not convincing anyone. James told John to take her home. There was no doubt in his mind now about what was wrong with her.

* * *

On Thursday of that week she came back to work, looking and feeling a little better. The tablets the doctor had given her were making her feel hungrier, so she was starting to eat more. It was important for her to build herself up, she reminded herself, so she mustn't forget to take them.

On Friday afternoon everyone started talking about going to the pub after work, as usual.

'You coming, Jim?' asked Tim when James came out of his room.

'Yeah,' he said.

'What about you, Lynsey?' Tim asked. 'Are you up to it?'

'Hold me back,' she said, noticing that James gave her an odd look. When he went back to his room she followed him in.

'OK, what is it now?' she asked.

'What do you mean?'

'Is there some reason I shouldn't go to The Bar for a drink after work?' she asked, beginning to get angry at his interference. He raised his eyebrows.

'What about Nick?' he asked, not wanting to mention her state of health directly.

'What's it got to do with Nick?' she threw back at him.

'Well, he's not going, is he? He won't be too happy if you go on your own, now that you're tying the knot.'

'Tying the knot?' she asked stupidly.

'Getting married. John told me at the Christening. Sorry, I suppose I shouldn't have said anything yet.'

'For your information,' she said tartly, 'Nick and I have finished, not that it's any of your business.' She turned and left his room, closing the door firmly behind her. She was glad she'd had an opportunity to tell James she was a free agent again, but she was furious with John. She took a long deep breath and headed back to her desk.

'You going to The Bar tonight, John?' she asked on the way past.

'Don't know,' he said.

'Under the thumb already, are we?' she said cunningly.

'Can do what I want,' he claimed stoutly.

At 5 o'clock he was the first to leave, throwing Lynsey's coat at her and pulling at her arm.

'Come on, slowcoach, let's go,' he said bossily. As they walked along the street, he gave her a quizzical look.

'You're awful quiet, sis, what's up?'

'Actually, I wanted a bit of a word with you, John,' she told him, pulling him into a shop doorway so the others couldn't see them. 'What the hell do you think you're playing at, telling James Bolton me and Nick are getting married!' she demanded, speaking through clenched teeth.

He took a moment to answer, then said carefully, 'I never said that. He must've got the wrong end of the stick.'

'John,' she said, exasperated, 'you know how you always know when I'm fibbing?'

'Yeah.'

'Well, it cuts both ways. Give it up. I want to know what you've got against him.'

'I'm just looking out for you, Lynsey. I don't want you to get hurt. He's not right for you.'

'Don't you dare make my decisions for me. I'm so mad at you, John, and you know what happens when I'm mad. I don't think I'm going to want to talk to you again for a long time—'

'Lynsey, don't get mad.'

'Too late,' she said, turning away from him.

'Please, Lynsey, I can't stand it when you won't talk to me.'

She folded her arms and put her head on one side as if she was considering things.

'I'll make it up to you, sis,' he promised rashly.

'You bet you will,' she told him, a little smile curling the corners of her mouth.

Lynsey made sure John knew what was expected of him before they joined the others in the pub. It was busy that evening and the guys were all standing in a group at the bar, trying to get served. After a couple of drinks, James was amused to hear Lynsey saying to John that she was really hungry. He hadn't heard her saying that for a long time. She dug at John's arm until he said, 'Oh, all right then.'

He announced loudly that he and Lynsey were going off to get some food.

'Anyone else coming?' he asked, looking at both Tim and James.

'No way,' said Tim, 'waste of good drinking time.'

'Actually, I'm quite hungry as well,' said James.

Lynsey had known he would say that, as he often skipped lunch these days.

'OK, come on then,' said John and the three of them headed out of the door. They walked along the road without speaking, each of them busy with their own thoughts. When they arrived at the Fish Bar, there was quite a long queue. They joined the end of it, but Lynsey kept complaining that she couldn't wait that long.

'Mmm, do you smell that pizza?' she said, closing her eyes and sniffing the appetising aroma from the Italian restaurant a couple of doors along.

'Well, we could always nip in there for pizza instead of standing out here in the cold,' said John. There was a funny edge to his voice and James frowned and looked at Lynsey.

'But that would take longer,' she pointed out.

'No it won't, I know one of the waiters,' said John.

'Well, that sounds like a plan to me,' Lynsey agreed. They both looked at James, who shrugged.

'You're sounding like more of a double act than Nick and Tim tonight,' he muttered. 'Come on, let's eat,' he added as he pushed open the restaurant door.

Twenty minutes later the three of them were seated at a table for four and had just been served their pizzas when James asked John which waiter he knew.

'Er, he doesn't seem to be in tonight actually,' John said sheepishly, looking rather relieved when his mobile rang.

'Bugger!' he said fiercely, and James gave him a speculative look. John answered the call in one-word replies, then shut it down with a snap and stood up.

'Gotta go,' he said, putting on his jacket again. 'Marcia.'

'What about your pizza – aren't you going to eat it first?' asked James in amazement.

'More than my life's worth. Marcia's climbing the walls. See you.' And he left, reluctantly, turning to give Lynsey a brooding look as he went out of the door.

James and Lynsey looked at each other and then put their heads down and sat and ate in silence for a moment. A waiter came and took John's plate away.

'I can't believe he went off like that,' said Lynsey, trying to look surprised.

'Yes, he's been behaving strangely tonight. A bit awkward, isn't it?' he added.

He looked at her for a few moments while she was preoccupied with her meal. She was wearing black trousers and a black top of soft jersey material that clung to her curves. But instead of looking sexy, the outfit made her look even paler and thinner than usual. The silver earrings and chain she usually wore would have brightened her appearance considerably, but she'd been too tired to bother with jewellery that morning.

He asked her why she wasn't drinking any alcohol, wondering how she would explain that, but she just smiled and so he smiled back at her. She told him he should smile more often. She was just wondering how to get started with what she wanted to say when she noticed he was now smiling at someone behind her, who had just come into the restaurant and was waving at him.

'Who's that?' Lynsey asked.

'Paul, a good friend of mine, and his girlfriend, Penny.'

They came over to speak to James and he introduced them to Lynsey.

'Great to see you, James, it's been ages,' said Paul, slapping James on the back.

'Mind if we join you?' Paul asked jovially.

James looked at Lynsey, who smiled.

''Course not,' she said, because she couldn't really do anything else. So Paul sat next to James and Penny sat beside Lynsey. *So much for talking*, thought Lynsey. She soon realised that Paul was not only very good-looking, he was very charming and sociable, too. In fact, he was complimenting her and chatting her up in no time!

'Where's James been hiding *you* then?' he asked her. James bristled and looked uncomfortable.

'Lynsey's a colleague, Paul,' he said stiffly, his eyes asking Paul to please shut up.

'Yeah, and I suppose this is a business dinner!' Paul scoffed.

'Paul, you're embarrassing them!' Penny said.

Paul just laughed, digging James in the ribs. James looked over at Lynsey, and was relieved to see she was smiling and didn't look at all put out. Paul went off to the Men's a little later and Penny told James and Lynsey that she and Paul had become engaged during the previous weekend.

'Congratulations!' said Lynsey. 'You seem well suited, but … don't you get mad at him when he flirts with other women?' she asked.

'No, not a bit,' Penny answered, laughing. 'That's just Paul being Paul.'

James nodded and just then Paul came back to the table.

'A tenner says you've been talking about me while I was gone!' he quipped, holding his hand out for the money. They all laughed and James slapped his hand.

'That's for us to know,' he retorted and they all laughed again.

The rest of the evening passed in the same way. The food was good and Paul and Penny were great fun to be with, and even though they were drinking only soft drinks because they were driving, Lynsey couldn't remember when she'd last had such a good time.

They said goodbye to Paul and Penny at the door a couple of hours later.

'You must come to our engagement party!' Paul said enthusiastically.

'Paul—' James began.

'We'd love to,' Lynsey put in quickly.

'We'll be in touch,' promised Paul as they waved goodbye.

James walked Lynsey to her car. They chatted about Paul and Penny and agreed they were a very nice couple. Lynsey was starting to yawn.

'It was a great evening, James,' she said as she got into her car.

'Yes it was. I enjoyed it, too. It's often the way when it's unexpected,' he replied.

'James—' she began, intending to ask him to come to her flat for coffee and a long talk, but he interrupted her.

'Goodnight, Lynsey, I'll see you on Monday,' he said curtly, heading off to his own car. *So much for that plan*, she thought sadly, and drove home slowly and miserably.

* * *

Things were a little easier between the two of them during the next week, but Lynsey still needed to have a proper heart-to-heart with him. She wanted to know if he was just attracted to her, or if he felt the same way she did, that they could have a future together. She was thinking about him constantly now and wondered if they really could put the past behind them. She hoped he felt the same way. She felt quite hopeful that they could patch things up between them, but then, following a weekend that seemed to last for ever, his mood unexpectedly took a turn for the worse.

On the Monday morning he came into the office slightly late, which was really unusual for him, and marched straight into his room without even saying 'Good morning' to anyone. He continued to behave like a bear with a sore head all day and she tended to keep out of his way when he was like that. It was rather puzzling, though, she thought, as he was in the process of moving into his brand new house and should be excited about it.

John went into James's room at lunch time to try to find out what was bugging him and he shrugged and told him it was just something silly. Then he seemed to relax a little. He took his scotch from the cabinet and poured them both a drink. John raised his brows and sipped the whisky, waiting for him to speak. James told him that he'd gone round to the house to get the last of his things and when he went round the back he looked at the garden and all his roses were dead. They'd obviously been poisoned and he added that it didn't take a genius to work out who had done it.

'What a bitch!' said John, who was genuinely shocked. 'What's she got to gain by doing that?'

'She knew they meant a lot to me. Just her parting shot, I suppose, something to remember her by,' James added sadly. 'As if I'm ever likely to forget what she's like!'

'Christ, it should be *you* being vindictive towards *her*, not the other way round.'

'Gina doesn't see things like that. I got away from her and cut her money supply off and she's not pleased.' He looked at John. I know they were only flowers, but it hurts like hell, John, it really does.'

'You're well rid, Jim, you know that, don't you?' John stated. He felt sorry for James, but he saw him as damaged goods, emotionally speaking, and as far his sister was concerned, he was more determined than ever to keep them apart. He went back into the main office and when he saw James heading for the toilets he went over to Lynsey's desk and told her what had happened, hoping that she would draw the same conclusions as he had about James.

'Best steer well clear for a while,' he warned.

She nodded, looking upset, and John felt reassured that things were going according to plan. Luckily, the previous week's detour to the restaurant hadn't resulted in them getting back together again, as far as he knew. He was determined that they never would be together again, but he was getting tired of keeping on top of it all the time. The best thing he could do, he decided, was try to persuade Lynsey to find another job and leave Forrest & Bolton for good.

Lynsey felt really low now, thinking about what Gina had done and wondering if his wife's viciousness had made James too cynical to want to put his trust in anyone again. It didn't bode well for the future and her decision to find out where she stood with him.

29

Engagement Party

The following day, Lynsey brought James's outgoing mail into his room for him to sign. He was speaking on the phone to Paul and he motioned her to stay. He was frowning as he spoke and then he looked at her rather sheepishly.

'Paul, I can't speak for Lynsey. I told you, she's a colleague. She's here now, I'll put her on and you can speak to her yourself,' he said, handing her the receiver.

'Hi, Paul,' she said, smiling, 'how are you doing?'

'Hi, gorgeous' he said easily. 'Just rang to make sure you two are coming to our "do" on Friday.'

'*This* Friday?' she asked.

'Yeah. Don't say you can't come because I'm not taking "no" for an answer!' he assured her.

She laughed. 'I'll be there, with bells on!' she replied, looking at James.

'Brilliant. About 7 on Friday then. See ya!'

'Give my love to Penny,' she said and passed the receiver back to James, who was looking pleased now.

'It's getting near the end of the month,' she said to him, thinking about her finances. 'Do you want to put together for a present for them?'

He nodded. 'Any ideas on what could we get for them?'

'There's a little shop in Quarry Street. Mostly antiques, but they've got more modern things, too—'

'I know, I go in there quite a lot!' he said.

'So do I,' Lynsey told him, 'sometimes just to look around. Will we go along there at lunchtime and see if they've got anything?'

'OK, let's do that,' he agreed, smiling.

At lunchtime, they had fun browsing round the little shop looking at the knick-knacks. They chose a clock which was in a modern style but quite decorative. They were both pleased with it.

'You can't go wrong with a clock,' said Lynsey. 'Even if they get two or three other clocks as gifts, you need quite a few for different rooms in the house, don't you?'

James agreed and they took it over to the till. The shopkeeper asked if it was a gift and then wrapped it for them, putting it in a really attractive bag with a gift tag attached. They went for a quick bite in a nearby café afterwards and then hurried back to work. A few eyebrows were raised when they came back into the office together, a little after 2 o'clock. John didn't look too pleased, but had enough sense not to say anything.

Lynsey was feeling so tired these days she decided to take Friday off, so on Thursday at home time James suggested that he pick her up on Friday evening at 6.30.

'No sense in us both taking our cars,' he said practically.

On the Friday evening, when she was finished getting changed and doing her make-up, Lynsey took the little gift bag out of the cupboard and wrote a message on the tag. *All the best from Lynsey and Jim*, she put in her best handwriting.

He arrived promptly at 6.30 and told her she looked lovely, which she did. She was wearing tight brown jeans with a slinky brown top of soft jersey material that clung to her curves. It had a fairly low cross-over neckline and little flared cap sleeves, and there was a subtle sparkle to it. It was very flattering and she felt good in it. She'd teamed it up with a gold pendant and long, narrow gold earrings that caught the light when she moved her head. Her hair had completely returned to its natural colour now and hung like a silky golden brown curtain around her shoulders. She had used an extra glosser on it and her straighteners, so she looked as if she had been to a salon. The overall effect was under-stated but very attractive and James found it difficult not to stare at her. He was aware, however, that she was not just slim now, she was getting quite thin, and her make-up didn't totally hide her pallor or the shadows beneath her eyes.

They sat for a while before they left, sipping soft drinks.

'Don't feel you can't drink just because I'm not,' James said, as if he was being considerate. He wondered how she would explain the not drinking, as she wasn't likely to tell him the real reason.

'I'll get something later,' she answered. 'Alcohol makes me flushed when I'm keyed up. I don't want to arrive looking like a Belisha beacon!'

He laughed and the tension eased a little. For something to do, he lifted up the gift bag and looked at the tag.

'Lynsey and Jim,' he murmured.

'Well, if you wanted Jim and Lynsey, you should have written it yourself!' she teased.

'It's just fine as it is,' he said quietly. It made him feel good to see their names together on the card.

'Shall we go?' he said, standing up and holding the door open for her.

* * *

They were first to arrive, which was good from the point of view that they got to choose the best seats. The lights were low in the lounge and Lynsey decided to risk a glass of wine. She wouldn't have any more after that, though, she decided. She had every intention of having a good long talk with James tonight and wanted to stay as sober as possible.

Paul and Penny were delighted with their gift and Paul read out the tag, giving James a meaningful look. James was glad when more guests arrived at the door at that point and the room soon filled up.

The party went with a swing, and Lynsey enjoyed dancing with James again. She realised it had been nearly a year since they'd danced together before, at last year's Christmas event.

Later in the evening, as they were beginning to dance to slower ballads, a young man about Lynsey's age, with long hair in dreadlocks, who said his name was Jaz, kept coming over and insisting that she dance with him. So she danced with him, hoping that would be the end of it, but she eventually had to tell him to leave her alone, as he wouldn't let go of her. She could see James in the background, sitting glowering at him. He stood up and came up behind Jaz.

'You heard, mate. Leave her alone,' he said menacingly.

Jaz turned around and looked him up and down, then he turned to Lynsey and said sneeringly, 'I didn't realise you'd brought your old man with you.' He let go of her wrist reluctantly and stalked off to annoy someone else.

Lynsey thanked James, but she could see that he was upset by that last remark and he sat quietly beside her for a while.

'You don't have to stick beside me, you know' he said to her, 'just because we arrived together.'

She put her drink down on the coffee table and said, 'Why don't we just leave now? I think the night's going to get worse rather than better and I've had enough anyway. How about you?'

He nodded and they lifted their jackets and went over to say their goodbyes to Paul and Penny.

'See you at the wedding,' Paul yelled as he waved them off at the door.

James drove her home, saying very little, and when they arrived at her flat she asked him to come in for coffee. He hesitated.

'I don't think so,' he said. 'It's late and we're both tired. I'll see you on Monday.'

He opened the door for her and she got out and walked along the path towards her flat. When she reached the top of the stairs, she turned round to wave, but he had gone already. She went inside and went into the lounge, sitting down on the settee in the dark, still wearing her jacket. She suddenly felt very tired and weary and just wanted to go to sleep, and she was also very disappointed. *The best laid plans*, she thought. The evening had come to nothing, all because of that stupid Jaz and his nonsense. James had seemed to have something weighing on his mind and was probably thinking that there was too much of an age gap between them and too much bad blood into the bargain. But she didn't think of him in terms of his age, she just thought of him as James, and she always would.

Maybe he simply didn't care enough to make the effort to put things right with her again. It seemed to be the nature of their relationship that when one of them wanted to move things forward, the other would back off. She sighed heavily and headed off to bed, another long weekend alone ahead of her. She was sick of this, she decided. Come Monday, she resolved, she was going to have it out with him once and for all.

30

High Noon

Lynsey came in to work on Monday in a very bad mood. She was still rather tired and low and couldn't stop fretting about the future. If she spoke to James and he wasn't interested, she would have to leave Forrest & Bolton and she would only see him again on very rare occasions, through his friendship with Jack and John. That prospect was really daunting, but she was going to have to risk it because she just couldn't go on like this any longer. There was so much she still didn't know about him, she thought, chewing on her bottom lip apprehensively. She wanted marriage, a home and children, as she always had, but now she realised she only wanted those things with him, not anyone else. But did *he*? And was he worth all the angst she was going through? Maybe he would just let her down again in the end. She was really tired of all the 'ifs', 'buts' and 'maybes' that were going through her mind.

She got through the day somehow and just as everyone was leaving and she was trying to steel herself for a confrontation with him, he rang her extension and asked her to come through to his room. She went in and closed the door.

'I was just about to ask if you had time for a talk,' she said nervously.

'Oh, what did you want to talk about?' he asked her.

'Oh, it'll keep. You first,' she said, putting it off as long as possible now that the moment was here and her courage was beginning to desert her. He asked her to sit down. He stood up and looked out of the window for a moment, fidgeting with the blinds, then he bit his bottom lip nervously and turned to face her.

'Lynsey, I know that things are difficult for you at the moment.'

She raised her eyebrows and he paused a second, then went on.

'But I want you to know that even though you and Nick are finished, you're not on your own.' She frowned and he sighed in exasperation. 'I'm not saying this right. It's not easy … the thing is, you can always marry *me*. You don't have to face it all by yourself.'

She was stunned and confused at the same time. 'Marry you? Face what? What do you mean?' she asked.

'You don't have to pretend – I know what's wrong with you.'

'Yes – what about it?'

He stared at her. 'This is serious, Lynsey. You can't just pretend it isn't happening. I know you told me to get lost before, but things are different now. I think, given time, we could really make a go of it. You're going to need help and support when the baby comes and I was hoping you would at least consider it …' he tailed off, feeling that he was losing the battle.

Lynsey's jaw had dropped and she closed it again. He'd just answered all her questions about him in one go, including how he felt about her, even though he hadn't said 'I love you' in so many words. She would have found it difficult, herself, to say that to *him* just then. Her throat seemed to close up every time she even thought about saying it, but that would come in time, she was sure, so long as the feelings were there. Her heart was starting to beat fast now and her brain was working even faster.

'Let me get this straight,' she said, getting up and walking over to him.

'You think I'm having Nick's child and so you want to marry me?'

'Yes – I mean no.'

'OK, let me put it this way,' she said. 'If you didn't think I was pregnant, you wouldn't be asking me to marry you?'

'No – I mean yes. It's not about the child. What I mean is, I know you're probably thinking I'm the last person you'd want to marry, after all that's happened, but I know you won't have a termination and you probably think you can manage fine on your own. And I'm not saying you can't, but—'

'Jim, before you go any further, there's a couple of things I need to clear up here. First of all, I am not pregnant—'

But – you must be. You've been so tired and not eating. You fainted the other day—'

'My haemoglobin's low,' she informed him.

He gave her a blank look.

'I'm anaemic. I need iron, that's all. I'm going to be just fine in a couple of weeks.'

He looked relieved, then disappointed and then embarrassed. 'Oh,' was all he could say.

'Second of all, I'd never get married for a reason like that. I wouldn't get married unless I felt so much for someone that I couldn't imagine life without them.'

'Oh,' he said again, feeling deflated.

'And third, I think we need to get to know each other a lot better before anybody starts even thinking about marriage.'

His eyes locked with hers, the frown lines straightened from his forehead and he swallowed hard.

'Lyns …' he began, moving towards her tentatively. She put up her hand to stop him coming any further.

'And another thing, you should know I have a zero tolerance for infidelity and dishonesty. Partly, I suppose, because of all the misery that came out of Jack's affair with my mother, and partly because it's just the way I am. So if it's not the way *you* are, then there's no point—'

'But it *is* the way I am, Lyns, it is. I've just never had a chance to prove it. It's just the way my life turned out. I didn't want it to be like that. All I ever wanted was to have a normal married life and a family—'

'Speaking of which,' she interrupted, moving closer to him and wrapping her arms around his neck, 'before you start talking about having children, bear in mind that twins tend to run in families, so you might be getting more than you bargained for!' She tilted her face up and drew his head down towards her.

It was some time before he lifted his head again. He caught sight of John standing by the front door, his lips pursed in annoyance and his arms folded across his chest. James gave him a broad grin and watched him turn and leave abruptly. He had already forgiven his friend for coming between the two of them, because now he had everything he wanted. Explanations about earlier misunderstandings would have to wait. He looked down at Lynsey and said happily, 'We've got a lot of talking to do, you and I.'

'I've got a better idea,' she replied, smiling up at him, 'let's do the talking later.'

'Yes,' he agreed with a grin,'much later!'

31

Day of Reckoning

In August of the following year, Lynsey Robson sat in a white limo beside her father, heading for the lovely old church where Kylie had been christened, and where she and James were going to be married. The driver had helped Jack into the car and had stowed his wheelchair in the boot. Father and daughter both sank back gratefully into the plush white leather upholstery. Jack favoured her with a beaming smile.

'This is the proudest day of my life, Lynsey,' he told her.

'I'm feeling quite pleased with myself, too,' she told him contentedly. 'But don't you go getting all slushy and making my mascara run, or you'll be in trouble,' she warned him, arranging her cream silk skirts about her so they wouldn't get crushed.

They soon arrived at the church and Lynsey climbed out carefully, then turned and helped Jack ease himself into his chair. As she pushed him along towards the door of the church, Jack became quite tense. His heart began to thump and the adrenaline started pumping. *I can't do this*, he thought, *what if I try and I can't do it? It's Lynsey's day. I don't want to muck it up, or steal her thunder.*

'Lynsey, could you stop for a moment before we go down the aisle?' he asked her.

'Of course,' she answered, smiling down at him. 'I have to arrange my dress properly, and I want to wait till 2 o'clock exactly – don't want James thinking I'm too keen!'

While she sorted her skirts and straightened her head-dress, Jack gently slid towards the edge of his chair, then braced himself, grasping both arms of the chair tightly, and slowly raised himself up. He'd done it quite a few times before, but this time his legs were shaking slightly, so it was a little more difficult. As Lynsey turned and saw what he was doing, she gasped and stood with her mouth open, gaping at him.

'No, Dad, you can't—' she began.

'I can do it if we walk very slowly,' he told her. 'I'm not taking my wee girl down the aisle in that thing, not if I can help it,' he said, glancing disparagingly at the chair. 'I've arranged for it to be brought forward beside the pew once I've given you away,' he told her. This reassured her a little, and she realised it wasn't the first time he had left his chair and walked. He held his arm out towards her and she took it very gingerly, praying that he would be all right.

As they walked very slowly down the aisle, people glanced round to look at the bride and then did a double-take as they saw Jack walking beside her. May was standing beside the aisle near the front on the bride's side of the church and she turned round to watch them and to give Jack an encouraging smile. She was holding little Kylie for Marcia, who was Lynsey's bridesmaid, and she felt very happy and proud. For a woman who had never given birth, she was now blessed with a stepson and daughter, a daughter-in-law and a granddaughter! *Not bad going*, she decided. As Jack and Lynsey passed her, she saw that Jack was feeling the same way. Pride oozed from every pore as he soaked up the shock and surprise on everyone's faces – everyone's, that is, except his wife's.

At first he hadn't wanted to tell her what was happening when the intensive physiotherapy started to strengthen his spine and his muscles, and he'd known that with a great deal of effort and determination, he would walk again. The specialist had warned him that his spine would never fully recover from the trauma of the crash; he would always need the aid of a walking stick and activities such as running and dancing were probably not on the agenda. But at least he wouldn't be confined to the wheelchair for the rest of his life.

He had wanted to surprise everyone, including May. Then he'd reconsidered. He was very wary of keeping anything from her now, even good news. As soon as he'd managed to stand up by himself, he'd told his wife, giving her strict instructions not to tell anyone else. He had learned his lesson well.

Lynsey also felt very emotional as they slowly made their way along the aisle. She could see James standing very straight and tense at the front of the altar, with John by his side. Explanations had been made between the two of them, man to man, and their friendship was stronger than ever now. She had never actually told James she loved him yet, even though she had agreed to marry him. This was because of the way he had treated her in the beginning; she needed him to understand that she would not allow him to mistreat her in any way. However, she would not leave things like that. She intended to assure him of the depth of her feelings when they were alone together after the reception. She didn't want the shadow of any misunderstandings or uncertainties between them at the start of their new life together.

She smiled to herself as she thought about the future and then she saw her mother standing a few rows from the altar. Tony was by her side and she was dabbing at her dry eyes very delicately with a tissue. Lynsey had at first intended to make Julia pay for her destructive behaviour by not inviting her to the wedding, but James had persuaded her that this would be wrong, and that in years to come it would bother Lynsey more than it would Julia. Jack had agreed with him and she had reluctantly capitulated. But she had decided that today was to be the day of reckoning for Julia nonetheless, and had considered at length how best to ensure that her mother paid for her past sins. There would be no confrontation, no marring of the wedding day. She knew that Julia had not told Tony about her bid to get Jack back, and she also knew that Julia did not really care about Tony but was simply using him, so she had laid her plans accordingly. Tony didn't deserve to be stuck with Julia, she decided, and Julia certainly didn't deserve someone like Tony!

* * *

Later that day, Lynsey Bolton was returning to the Function Room after changing into her 'going away' outfit when she spotted Tony on his own, coming out of the Men's room. She walked over to him, smiling, and thanked him for coming. Then she drew him aside and, after carefully checking that Julia was nowhere in sight, had a quiet little chat with him. He said nothing while she spoke, merely nodding and pursing his lips. When she finished speaking, he went off to look for Julia and Lynsey went to find James. It was time for them to leave.

* * *

As they stood together waving back at everyone and smiling for the photographer, James could see Julia standing alone, a little apart from the crowd. She looked very annoyed about something and there was no sign of Tony. James turned towards his bride.

'Lyns, what have you been up to?' he asked.

'What goes around comes around, so they say,' she answered non-committally.

'So, I'm not destined for a quiet life then?' he said, on a sigh of acceptance, as he stood back to let her climb into the limo before him.

She just smiled sweetly at him and batted her eyelashes, and as the car drove off, they put their arms around each other. She looked at him and realised that she didn't even care any more about Julia's misdemeanours or anything else – the only thing she cared about now was being with James.

'I love you, James,' she whispered into his ear. She saw tears come into his eyes, so she added, 'as long as you behave yourself!'

and that made him laugh. Tears and laughter together should make a rainbow, she thought happily, and there would be a few rainbows on the horizon for the two of them, if Lynsey had anything to do with it.

THE END